His che

her perfume and the scent of her skin.

"Oh, Luc." Olivia raised her head and took a deep breath. The luminescent aqua of her eyes held him enthralled, but he wouldn't rush and risk losing her when he'd just found her again. Whispering French endearments against her hair, he waited for a hint of an invitation.

Years of frustrating loneliness flipped through his mind as he mentally urged her to come to him, to relax in his arms. She clasped her fingers around his nape and he claimed her mouth in a searing kiss, the kiss he'd given her a thousand times in his fantasies. Parting her lips, his tongue explored and played and tasted as he molded her lithe form against him.

How he wanted her. She moaned and clung to his neck, returning his kiss with the same passion that had set him on fire in the past. He was home now, with Olivia in his arms. There was hope for them.

His lips glided along her cheek, and he tucked a strand of hair behind her ear. "I am so glad you invited me. I will protect you and Melissa. Everything will be fine. I will help you get rid of your fears. I promise." Things would work out, and in time, they would inform Melissa of the truth about her father.

For a crazy moment, Olivia tried to believe him, to imagine she could spend the rest of her life in his arms and make up for the time wasted away from him for her daughter's sake... Now Melissa was sixteen, soon to have her own life.

Olivia touched her swollen lips, hesitating. *Kiss him. You'll talk later.* But she wouldn't lie now. No matter what it cost, she couldn't let him build dreams based on a lie.

Praise for *Prescription for Trust*

"Mona Risk's PRESCRIPTION FOR TRUST is really a prescription for a steamy reunion romance with loads of mystery and a French doctor to die for. Ms. Risk is known for her talent of writing sexy foreign heroes and the angsty heroines they can't live without. Luc and Olivia are perfect for each other and PRESCRIPTION FOR TRUST is just what the doctor ordered."

~Carla Capshaw, 2004 and 2007 Golden Heart winner, *The Heart Beckons*

"Another compelling novel by Mona Risk, PRESCRIPTION FOR TRUST is a page-turner packed with intrigue, romance and heart-twisting emotion!"

~ Stacey Kayne, RT Reviewer's Choice Nominee

"Olivia's heart-wrenching experience as a mother who gives up love to protect her child and Luc's relentless effort to save the woman he loves from endless guilt will captivate you from the first page to the satisfying conclusion. The wonderful characters and emotional situations make this book a keeper."

~Helen Scott-Taylor, *The Magic Knot*
2008 *Romantic Times* winner

***PRESCRIPTION FOR TRUST* awards:**

First Place in Central Ohio *Ignite the Flame*

Second Place in Heart of Denver, *The Molly*

Third Place in FTHRW *Golden Gateway*

Dear Marion
Happy reading
Mona Risk
Oct. 20, 2010

Prescription for Trust

Doctor's Orders, Book 1

by

Mona Risk

This is a work of fiction. Names, characters, places, and incidents either are the product of the author's imagination or are used fictitiously, and any resemblance to actual persons living or dead, business establishments, events, or locales, is entirely coincidental.

Prescription for Trust: Doctor's Orders, Book 1

Contact Information: info@thewildrosepress.com

Cover Art by Tamra Westberry

The Wild Rose Press
PO Box 708
Adams Basin, NY 14410-0706
Visit us at www.thewildrosepress.com

Publishing History
First Champagne Rose Edition, 2009
Print ISBN 1-60154-631-9

Published in the United States of America

Dedication

My deepest thanks to:

My editor Kat O'Shea for her continuous help.

Tamra Westberry, the artist who created my beautiful book cover.

My critique partners Helen Scott-Taylor and Joan Leacott for their endless reading.

Stacey Kayne, Roxanne St. Claire and Anna Sugden for offering invaluable advice.

The psychiatrists and physicians who suggested, read and corrected medical cases. I couldn't have written this book without their expert opinions.

Paul and Zina for brainstorming with me.

Sam for sharing my stress and joys.

This book is dedicated to my mother who has been a mentor, a friend and a shining example of courage and perseverance.

Other books by Mona Risk:

Babies in the Bargain

Coming soon from the Wild Rose Press
as part of the Doctor's Order series:

Prescription for Hope
Prescription for Love
Prescription for Change

Chapter One

"Olivia, why didn't you tell me you knew Dr. Vicour-Michelet?" Bypassing morning greetings, the Chairman of Psychiatry, Dr. Herb McMillan, never wasted precious minutes on the phone.

"I don't." Tapping the faded, old desk in her windowless office, Dr. Olivia Crane scoured her mind to put a face to the name. "Never met him. But I read his articles, the ones you passed on to me. He seems like a brilliant psychiatrist. I'm sure he'll be an excellent addition to our department." Maybe she'd be able to sleep a little more than four hours with the French doctor on board for six months.

Doc cleared his throat then paused as if to choose his words. "When I sent him your enthusiastic report last Thursday, he e-mailed back on Friday that he'll be here on Sunday. And *voilà*, as he said."

"*Voilà*, what?"

"He arrived last night."

"Already? He wasn't supposed to be here for two more weeks." With her busy schedule, Olivia hadn't had time to check the visiting physician's website yet.

A soft chuckle sounded on the other line. "The first thing he told me was he couldn't wait to see you."

To see...me? Why? Olivia blinked.

Doc kept mumbling in her ear as she pulled one of their visitor's articles from the pile on her desk and punched his website into her computer.

The name Vicour-Michelet flashed on the

screen, along with a photo that stopped her heart. A perfect, amazing picture of Luc.

Her Luc.

The picture didn't make sense. How had Luc ended up with such an incredibly long and aristocratic name?

Olivia zoomed in on the photo by two hundred percent. With the cursor, she traced blue eyes framed by dark lashes, chiseled nose and smiling lips.

"Dr. Lucien...de...Vicour-Michelet." Squinting at the screen, she studied Luc's handsome features. He was here? In Cincinnati? "Oh no."

"Yes," Doc replied, his voice excited. She heard a faint, "I'll bring him over."

The phone slipped from her sweaty palm and banged on the desk.

Olivia had welcomed the opportunity to co-author an article with a brilliant psychiatrist to further her career. But she was expecting an older, distinguished physician, Dr. L. de Vicour-Michelet, probably graying or bald.

Not drop-dead gorgeous Luc whose image was woven intimately into her most sensual dreams.

Darn. Luc might imagine she was behind the decision to invite him back to the Cincinnati University Hospital. Too late now for the chairman to politely withdraw the invitation.

An insistent beeping caught her attention. She reached for the receiver and put it back in its cradle.

Ten years was a long time. Maybe he was married. Her throat constricted. *God, I hope he doesn't come here with a wife and family.*

Her gaze frozen on the screen, Olivia couldn't tell how long she remained at her desk, staring at the monitor where Luc's picture smiled at her.

Someone knocked. Her office door opened. She bolted out of her chair, took a step, and stopped in her tracks. Doc came in, and towering behind him...Luc George.

Her pulse raced, her knees wobbled, her head swam. She stared at him, hands clenched behind her back to conceal their trembling.

With confident strides, Luc passed Dr. McMillan and circled her desk. A wide grin on his face, he halted in front of her, his hair mussed with a strand across his forehead, his eyes as bright as a cloudless sky. She recognized the amber and spice scents of his favorite cologne. The evocative fragrance transported her back to a time when she still believed love could work miracles.

"Olivia." His voice was hoarse. Different.

Awareness clicked in her foggy mind. She had to welcome him, a physician greeting a visiting colleague. She stiffened and extended her arm for a handshake.

Ignoring her hand, Luc cradled her shoulders. In a swift motion, he brought her against him and kissed her three times on the cheeks—right, left, and right again—in the French way. His lips left fiery spots where they touched her face, and her heart skipped a beat. She stepped back.

"Olivia," Luc repeated with a devastating smile.

"Luc?" Heat radiated to her throat, her chest, her belly.

Beyond the desk, Doc cleared his throat a couple of times.

Good grief, what was happening to her? Ten years of perfect control threatened to crumble in a few minutes.

What a mess. Lord, what a gigantic mess.

Luc's sparkling smile faded as he released her.

"Welcome to Cincinnati," Olivia said for the sake of saying something until she could recover her mental faculties.

"It is such a pleasure to be here again. I

appreciate the invitation." Luc's baritone voice sounded natural now, tinged with eagerness, in spite of his formal stilted English. She'd forgotten how he pronounced the *R* from deep in the throat and avoided contractions. "*Merci.*" He inched closer.

"You're welcome. Our department needs your expertise." She retreated a few more steps and flattened against the wall, unable to move or breathe. Luc held her gaze as if he'd come all the way from Paris to indulge in this agreeable pastime. Would he stop invading her space? "Excuse me."

Luc backed up and turned. He paused as his gaze fell on her computer screen displaying his enlarged picture. His lips curled into a satisfied smile. "Oh *chérie*."

Oh cripes. Her gaze flicked to the monitor screen and then settled back on Luc, a warm blush invading her cheeks.

A knowing grin spread across his face, and he squeezed her hand. "You don't have to be embarrassed," he whispered. "I missed you too."

No, please. The words lodged in her throat as she studied the man she'd once loved. The mischievous twinkling in the blue depth of his eyes, the contented smile, and the confident stance showed her in no uncertain terms Luc believed she'd called him back.

Standing so close to her sexy visitor did strange things to her usual composure. Unwelcome tremors fluttered through her body.

"Wait." She steadied herself, not wanting to convey the wrong signal. "You don't understand."

Dr. McMillan cleared his throat. "I haven't had my morning coffee yet." Her mentor's inquisitive gaze flipped from her to Luc. "Care to join me?"

"*Avec plaisir*. My pleasure," said Luc.

"Olivia?" Doc's eyebrow rose in an arch. "I'm sure you can use a freshly brewed cup. Strong. The way you like it."

Yes, she badly needed coffee. Grateful for the distraction, she nodded and squared her shoulders, eager to escape Luc's proximity and familiar scent.

****

When Olivia held the door open for him and Dr. McMillan, Luc suppressed an amused grin. His gaze rested on her hands. No ring there. She was still unattached, an independent, efficient woman, but her gesture defied his sense of chivalry.

"*Après toi*." Luc indicated she should pass in front of him. She glanced at him, her lips parting in an adorable smile, but she didn't question his good manners as she waited for him to follow her and then locked her door.

He'd wondered if he'd find her changed. Her perfume had. Still French. But heady and mature. Probably *Arpège*, stronger than the *Chanel* he'd given her years ago.

And her hair was different. She'd cut the long dark ponytail he used to wrap around his hand. Shoulder-length curls with blond streaks framed her face now. She was as lovely as he remembered, in a black pantsuit and light-green silk blouse that matched the aqua color of her eyes. A cool, serene Grace Kelly beauty. An impossible dream suddenly materializing. Olivia had been worth the wait. When would he be able to take her in his arms and taste the passion he'd missed so much?

"You guys go ahead." McMillan's voice snapped Luc out of his pleasurable contemplation. "I have to stop in my office. I'll join you in a minute."

"Let's walk outside. It's so gorgeous today." Olivia preceded Luc toward the hallway and the front door. She strolled out into the narrow road joining the School of Medicine to University Hospital.

Luc adjusted to Olivia's quick step. He'd walked

this path so often, ten years ago, fingers entwined with Olivia's, on the way to clinical rounds at the hospital or to breaks in the cafeteria.

The flowerbeds along the sidewalk overflowed with red, pink and white roses. Breathing the delightful autumn freshness, he glanced at Olivia. Was she sharing the same nostalgia?

"It is so good to be in Cincinnati, away from the grayness of Paris." And even better to have been called here by Olivia Crane, the woman who'd filled his fantasies for so long. He hoped this invitation was Olivia's graceful way to bring him back into her life. "I was happy to have finally heard from you after such a long time."

"Huh? I didn't...I mean I wasn't the one who wrote the invitation."

"I know, but you evaluated my articles. Thank you for the first-class recommendation."

"Oh." She glanced at him, then shrugged and appeared to study the roses. "The articles were very good."

"To be honest, I was hoping you would write or call sooner. You have only e-mailed me three times. And that was more than three years ago." He snorted. "Do you realize, Dr. Crane, that your last notes were mostly medical reports without a personal comment or question?" He gave her a sidelong glance.

Had she even noticed that his last name had changed two years ago? Probably not. She'd never questioned him about it and used the same address. Her e-mails had eventually stopped. To think of it, she'd also conspicuously missed the medical conferences he'd attended in the U.S.

She shook her head and sighed. "Come on, Luc. We exchanged e-mails for seven years before we decided to quit."

"*You* decided."

"We said good-bye once and for all, years ago." Without looking at him, she raised her chin in the stubborn way he recalled too well and accelerated her pace.

"But you promised you would call."

"Only if I needed help." She shrugged, indicating she'd managed well on her own, so far.

Damn her independent spirit, her assertive tone that shut him out and constricted his chest.

Then why had she asked him back through McMillan's invitation? What did she want from him?

Her smooth forehead and blank expression revealed none of her feelings. He longed to take her in his arms, melt her cool composure and hear her brazen moans. Old memories popped up, causing his muscles to tighten.

All in time, Lucien. He clenched and unclenched his fingers as he struggled to soothe his frustrated mind and cool his overheating body. Right now, he was happy to be with her again.

"Did you have a good trip?" Olivia asked, without slowing her steps.

"Great." He didn't mind the mundane conversation. Later, there would be plenty of time for intimate subjects. "McMillan was at the airport to receive me. He insisted I should stay at his house for the next three months."

"In a way you'll be doing him a favor. He's leaving for California in a couple days. Did he mention you'll have to feed the two dogs?" She tilted her head, green sparkles dancing in her eyes with barely concealed irony.

He chuckled. "I did not see any dogs last night."

"They were probably locked in the basement. Trust me I've often house-sat for the McMillans. A fabulous mansion in Indian Hill, but a lot of responsibilities."

"In that case I will count on you to help me." He

stepped closer. His blood raced with anticipation as he mulled over asking her to share the accommodation and chores with him.

"I don't have much time on my hands with Doc teaching at Berkeley during his sabbatical." Her cold tone left no doubt she'd understood his meaning and cut him right off.

Patience, Lucien. This was Olivia strolling next to him. At long last.

Difficult to believe. His Olivia.

Not one of the gorgeous women who'd paraded on his arm over the years. Staying away from her for so long had only reinforced his desire for her. Forgotten tingles spiraled through his gut. He wanted her back in his arms. Soon.

As they entered the cafeteria, the aroma of a hearty American breakfast wafted in the air. McMillan joined them at the buffet line. Luc loaded his tray with pancakes, eggs and sausage. Olivia chose a yogurt and a cup of coffee from the wide variety of items arranged on the counters.

They settled at a table near the wall. Luc attacked his pancakes with a hearty appetite, while Olivia spooned her yogurt ever so slowly, as if she planned to spend the whole day eating that small cup. *Bon Dieu*, with her figure, she didn't need to watch her diet.

A throaty grumble came from the next chair. "Dr. Lucien—"

"Please call me Luc, the nickname I use in the U.S."

McMillan chuckled. "It's your last name that trips up my tongue. I can't get myself to remember the dozen syllables."

"My name used to be Luc George when I joined the University of Cincinnati, ten years ago."

"So, you two knew each other then?" McMillan rubbed his chin, his gaze flitting from Luc to Olivia.

Luc raised his eyebrows and studied the very quiet Olivia. Her fingers flexed on her coffee cup. She turned her head toward the crowd invading the cafeteria, ignoring him.

Luc felt compelled to explain. "Olivia and I met at CUH during the year I spent here, specializing in sexual abuse disorders."

"I see. It must have been during the time I spent in England. But you never returned, right?"

"No, not to Cincinnati. I had no specific reason until you invited me." Luc shot a quick look at McMillan, then his gaze settled on Olivia's profile.

Why had she called him back?

Her chest rose, straining against the silk blouse, as she glanced sideways. Luc moistened his lips. When would he be able to have a private moment with her?

"But you often came to America according to your résumé." McMillan frowned while forking up his eggs.

With effort, Luc shifted his attention away from his gorgeous companion to concentrate on McMillan's comment. "I have given seminars at various conferences in New York, San Francisco, and Houston, and I spent time as a visiting physician at Columbia and Northwestern," he recited, wishing McMillan would get paged away.

Olivia turned toward Luc, her aqua eyes wide in surprise. "And you've agreed to come to UC?"

"Of course." How could she doubt that the University of Cincinnati would top the Ivy League universities in his mind? "In a way UC is my alma mater too."

An endearing flush spread across her cheeks. His fingers itched to caress her slender neck, and he longed to trail kisses along her delicate jaws. He dug his nails into his palms and smiled at her. Years ago, he'd memorized every inch of her satiny skin, every line and curve.

As soon as they could be alone, he'd convince her that his feelings had not changed. In fact, they'd amplified tenfold over the years.

McMillan pushed out his chair and stood. "I've an important appointment about a grant for our department. Luc, maybe you can go with Olivia and re-familiarize yourself with our Crisis Center."

Olivia's wary gaze flew toward McMillan. "I have a patient in fifteen minutes. Luc is probably tired from yesterday's long trip."

"Not at all. I slept all night long. I would rather start my job right away and sit in with you during your patient's visit, if you do not mind."

She hesitated, then shrugged. "Sure."

He focused on her face, puzzled by her frown and the thin line of her lips. She wouldn't have shared their past relationship with her boss, so she'd feel forced to curb her emotions in McMillan's presence. Luc refrained from any comments until they dropped off their trays and McMillan left.

"We should get going then," she said.

Luc motioned for her to lead the way. As they strode toward the Crisis Center, he asked, "Olivia, McMillan does not know?"

"Know what?" Her beautiful eyes narrowed in suspicion.

"About us."

"Of course not. I don't share personal matters with my colleagues or my boss." She looked away and climbed the stairs of the Crisis Center.

Luc followed her, his gaze fixed on her rigid spine. She wasn't acting the way he'd expected. No lingering smile, no enthusiastic words, not even eye contact to allow him to glimpse her feelings.

A memory played in his mind. The awful night she'd told him to go home and forget about her. She'd had that same mutinous and frustrated look.

Something was wrong.

As they entered the consultation room, Luc slipped his hand into his blazer pocket and fingered the official letter. McMillan had issued the invitation because the Department of Psychiatry needed Luc's expertise. And Luc, who wanted firsthand experience of the differences between American and French methods in psychiatric evaluation, had also agreed to coauthor the *Diagnostic Manual of Mental Disorders* with his American colleagues.

What about Olivia? She was the enigma that challenged him. Hoping she was interested in rekindling a passion he'd never been able to forget, he tried to stifle the doubt that slithered into his mind.

Would she have recommended him if she didn't want him in her life now?

Chapter Two

"Patricia, you hit your husband with a frying pan containing boiling oil?" Olivia suppressed a frown. In her seven-year career as a psychiatrist, she'd heard thousands of crazy stories in this consultation room.

Her hands flattened on the arms of her chair as she glanced at Luc. He nodded imperceptibly. A practiced consultant, he sat in a corner so he wouldn't disturb her patient with an extra presence, and listened without interfering.

The shy, jittery woman, slumped into a chair next to Olivia, raised her hands in a what-else-could-I-do gesture. "No, not hot. The damn pan'd been sitting for a while. It wasn't even warm, for crying out loud." Patricia scooted to the edge of her chair, laced her fingers together and twisted them. "He banged me on my head. Then he threw me on the floor. I wanted to get rid of him."

"I understand, Patricia. You were defending yourself." Olivia's heart went out to the abused patient.

"He said he'd take my baby. He'd never let me see him." Her eyes filling with tears, Patricia pressed her fist against her mouth. Her gaze flickered around the room like a trapped animal and settled on the door as if she feared someone might burst through it. "My husband is a butcher, way too brutal. His punches could have killed my Andy."

"Believe me, Patricia, I understand." Olivia considered her with sympathy. *I understand more than you could ever imagine.* "You were defending your son when you hit your husband."

"He turned around and took a can of beer from the fridge. My jaw hurt so much. And my ear. But I got up. I grabbed the pan and hit him on the head. He just dropped to the floor." The woman hugged herself and closed her eyes. Her whole face shrank into a wrinkled mask of fear.

"You were very brave to retaliate." Olivia pursed her lips. Her head tilted, she surveyed the six framed diplomas hanging on the wall as a reminder of her accomplishments.

She'd worked hard to become a respected psychiatrist, but long ago she hadn't had the courage to hit back. As she lowered her head, her gaze met Luc's. She read a question in his arched eyebrows, a disturbing thought that threatened her well-practiced control. Schooling her expression, she focused her attention on her patient. "You saved yourself."

"I had to get away. For Andy. He's only two." The woman shook her head as tears flooded her eyes.

"Good for you." Olivia knew firsthand to what lengths a mother would go to protect her child. She nodded to her patient. "We're here to help you."

"I'm terrified. I can't sleep at night. I keep holding Andy. I've been in counseling for several months."

"Do you live alone?"

"No, I shared an apartment with another abused woman, but she moved out of state. I couldn't stay on my own. Now, I'm back at the shelter for battered women where I hid two years ago. I never go out. I'm afraid to leave the house. The social worker brought me here. Soon, I'll have to make a decision about my future." The patient buried her head in her hands and sobbed. "But I can't leave. I can't be on my own. He'll find us and kill me."

After spending an hour questioning her patient, Olivia put a soothing hand on the young woman's arm. "Patricia, I'm going to give you a medicine called *Fluoxetine* to calm your anxiety."

Olivia explained the risks, benefits and side effects of the medicine, and then she handed Patricia a prescription and a consent form. "Take one in the morning only. I hope you'll start feeling better in a couple of weeks and you'll be able to discuss your future with the social worker with a cool head. Do you have any questions?"

Patricia shook her head and signed the printed sheet.

"I'll see you next week," Olivia said as she walked her out of the consultation room. When she resumed her place, Olivia turned toward Luc. "A case of post-traumatic stress disorder and agoraphobia."

"I agree with you. The antidepressant drug is appropriate for her case. But—" His gaze intense, Luc narrowed his eyes as if he wanted to reach deep in her soul.

"Yes?"

"I share your empathy toward an abused patient, but you seemed to approve of her violent reaction to her husband."

Had she been too transparent? She hoped not. No one knew her well. Not Luc or Doc, or even her daughter or her best friend, Tony. No one knew everything about her. And frankly, even she had almost forgotten the part of her life she'd buried deep down.

Luc had told her he detested secrets, but her life was a canvas of secrets woven to protect her child. She willed down her nervousness and shrugged. He wouldn't have understood her fears.

How would he react when he discovered she had a daughter? When he learned she'd never trusted him enough to tell him about Melissa ten years ago?

Damn it, she couldn't have trusted any man at the time.

With a psychiatrist of Luc's caliber looking over her shoulder, she'd have to watch her reactions. "I just wanted Patricia to talk without fear."

Olivia didn't need a shrink to tell her she was a good doctor, dedicated to her career, aggressive and not easily flustered. But when it came to her secret and her daughter's happiness, she was totally vulnerable, a mother afraid to see her daughter hurt, a woman feeling guilty about her past, unable to escape the web of secrets she'd created.

"For a moment I thought you'd lost your objectivity." His stern expression relaxed. "I must have been mistaken." His gaze rested on her face with a softness that worried her even more than his perceptiveness.

These next six months promised to be stressful. She glanced at her watch. "Doc must be done with his appointment. I wonder if he got his grant."

"You call him Doc?"

"An old habit I can't lose. He was my professor in med school."

Luc took a step toward her, the bone-melting smile she remembered too well curving his lips. "I like old habits. Olivia, I am glad we have a few minutes of privacy to talk about the past." He reached for her shoulders.

Her heart flip-flopped at his gentle but firm touch. Her skin burning under the silk blouse, she stared at him, unable to move.

"*Ma chérie,*" he murmured.

When you feel stressed, take a deep breath and count to ten, she'd often advised her patients. Hell, she wouldn't have time to reach ten. Luc was going to kiss her. Here in the psychiatric consultation room. Total madness.

"Luc, please. Doc is waiting." She ducked under his arms to escape his hold.

As if on cue, her cell phone rang. Doc. Bless his heart. For once, he'd called her at the right time. "Yes, Doc. I'm done here."

"Good. I need you both in my office. I have an important case to discuss with you."

"Can it wait till tomorrow, please?" She threw a look at Luc who was listening to every word. "I had other plans for this afternoon."

"Sorry about that. It's too important to wait."

"I see. In that case, I'll drop by for a moment."

"Can you postpone your plans? My wife just called. We'd like you to have dinner with us."

"I really can't." She hadn't been to her mother's house to see her daughter for three days.

"It's Luc's first night in Cincinnati. Your presence will help put him at ease."

"But—" Olivia stifled a curse. Luc was already more at ease than she'd ever be in his presence. The man oozed self-confidence and authority, whereas she'd forgotten how to be assertive in the last few hours.

"Please, Olivia. There are things to discuss with Luc before I can start my sabbatical. You know perfectly well that there isn't enough time during the day. Consider it a business meeting."

A business meeting? She sighed. Doc was leaving soon. He was right. They needed to brief Luc, but their workdays overflowed with patient consultations and classes. "Okay, I'll be there for dinner," she conceded grudgingly.

"Any problems?" Luc asked with his most charming smile.

"Just discussing dinner arrangements. Doc's expecting us. Let's go." She grabbed her purse and jacket, and exited the room while slipping an arm into the sleeve. Luc immediately held the jacket for her. Her heart squeezed. He hadn't changed. He was still the perfect gentleman.

"I wonder what's bothering Doc about this big case to call us *stat*?" As if she didn't have enough trouble with her visiting doctor and the gigantic misunderstanding of his invitation.

"A new, difficult case, maybe. He is leaving soon and has to transfer his responsibilities."

She nodded and walked the small distance between the Crisis Center and the School of Medicine in silence, struggling to keep her rising nervousness in check. A whiff of antiseptic and alcohol assailed her as she entered the School of Medicine building. Olivia had lived with this smell a third of her life, but for the first time it made her nauseous.

How would she extricate herself from the problem Luc's arrival had created?

Tonight, after dinner, once he'd settled in the McMillan's mansion, she'd tell him that nothing had changed. Nothing except his name.

"Where did you get this *Lucien de Vicour-Michelet*?"

"Two years ago, I inherited the lands, *château*, and title from my uncle on my mother's side. In his *testament*, he asked I use his name also."

"Title? So what do they call you in France? Monsieur what?" For her, he'd always been Monsieur Handsome. Just like now, drop-dead gorgeous in a collared shirt that reflected the blue of his eyes and contrasted with his wavy, dark hair.

"*Comte* de Vicour-Michelet."

"Oh dear, a count." The title suited his physique. An athletic and muscular body plus a scientific mind. *Oh, la, la.* A perfect fit for French aristocracy. Excitement sizzled in her stomach. She accelerated her pace to escape his gaze, his scent, his presence.

Nothing had changed. She'd hurt him years ago,

and she'd have to hurt him again.

****

"Come in, my friends. Make yourself comfortable." With a sly smile indicating he had more to say, Doc waved to the big leather chairs by his desk. "I have great news to share. Soon we'll be able to renovate the Crisis Center."

"Really?" Olivia returned his smile while she settled in a chair, and Luc did the same. Modernizing the Crisis Center had been the ongoing dream of every psychiatrist at the Center. "Has the dean signed your petition for more funds?"

"Nope, but we received a generous donation. Our benefactor opened a new branch of his company here a few months ago. He's just donated millions to the University of Cincinnati. And he specified the bulk of his money should go to our department."

"No way? Who would believe there still are such generous people in the world?" Relaxing against the back of her chair, Olivia shook her head in awe. "What a great man. Giving millions without asking for anything in return."

"Uh..." Shifting in his chair, Doc opened the file on his desk. "There is a stipulation. Our benefactor expects us to treat his grandson. The young man suffers from antisocial personality disorder with tendency to violence. You can find a report from his former psychiatrist in San Francisco. The patient has moved here at his grandfather's request."

Doc turned the folder around for Olivia and Luc to read.

A picture fluttered down. A man with blond hair and pale blue eyes. Late-thirties, handsome and arrogant. A face Olivia had hoped and prayed she'd never see again.

The smile on her lips turned into a bitter stretch as she lowered her head and glared at the face threatening her peace of mind.

God, Jeremy was in Cincinnati. So close. Olivia suppressed a shudder.

She'd left him in Chicago, seventeen years ago, and run away to hide in the heart of Ohio. At the time, he was about to graduate and work in his family's business in San Francisco. As far as possible from her.

And now he was here. *Here*?

The blood froze in her veins. Panicked, she glanced at the door, afraid she'd see it yanked open, revealing the monster from her past.

Breathing slowly to steady her heartbeat, she read the previous diagnosis through blurry eyes and tried to make sense of the words. *Antisocial personality disorder with tendency to violence.* Violence, all right. She'd experienced it firsthand. Apparently, Jeremy hadn't changed.

"Five million from Rutherford Senior to our Department of Psychiatry. Imagine what we can do with that money," Doc mused.

"Interesting case," Luc mumbled as he turned the page. He could read to his heart's content, but that was as far as she would get involved in Jeremy's case.

Straightening in her chair, she schooled her expression. "I can't handle that case."

"What?" Doc stared at her, his eyes wide.

"I can't handle it. Sorry. He needs someone more qualified on violence symptoms."

"What do you mean you're not qualified to handle this case, Dr. Crane?" Behind his desk, Doc lurched up from his wing chair, his face an indignant red.

"I..." Clearing her throat, she improvised a plausible reason. "I'm not familiar with some of his symptoms." Having studied Jeremy's symptoms in many patients, she almost snorted at her own lie.

Both Doc and Luc stared at her, their gazes

mirroring their disbelief. She shrugged, determined to avoid any pressure on their parts.

"That's bullshit, and you know it." Doc tapped his knuckles on the desk. The light rap resonated in the stern silence, grating on Olivia's ears even more than her mentor's caustic tone.

Luc crossed his arms, studying her as if she lay on the traditional psychiatric couch.

Keeping her impatience in check, she curled her lips in a half smile. "I usually deal with the victim, not the aggressor." She had the right to refuse a patient if there was conflict of interest. A humongous one. But she wasn't about to unveil her reasons to her boss and their visitor.

Arching a bushy brow, Doc raked his fingers through his grayish hair. "A patient is a patient."

"No." Jeremy Rutherford was not her usual patient.

"What's the big deal about this one?"

Staring at Doc, she sucked in a deep breath and debated her options.

Patience was not Doc's forte. "Well?"

A glance at the picture morphed into a glare as she traced the full lips and seductive smile and then gritted her teeth. She would not treat *this* patient if she were the last psychiatrist in town.

"All we need is your evaluation for him to be cleared of abuse charges," Doc continued in a persuasive tone.

Cleared of abuse charges? If she agreed to a consult, she'd expedite Jeremy straight to hell. Better still, she'd make sure he spent the rest of his corrupt and worthless life locked in jail or a mental institution. Olivia dug her nails into the leather arms of the chair and stamped a blank expression on her face. "I can't take him on."

Luc, who'd remained silent during the exchange, leaned forward, his elbow resting on his knees, his fingers tented against his chin. “Why? Any personal reason?”

Olivia flipped her gaze toward him. “Professional ethics.”

He raised his eyebrow. “I trust you are always perfectly objective?”

She knew he was referring to her empathy for the battered Patricia. Darn it, but he was more trouble than she’d anticipated, his perceptive eyes reading her like no one else. She fixed him with the gaze she’d perfected over the last five years, that cold gaze her students and residents had learned to respect and fear.

“I always do what’s best for my patients.” She pursed her lips, daring him to contradict her. The last thing she needed now was Luc’s insight into something she’d vowed to keep to herself.

He narrowed his eyes. Inquisitive sparkles glittered in the dark blue, threatening her peace of mind.

Doc cleared his throat. “Olivia, for heaven’s sake. This patient is particularly important. I need your help.”

“I really can’t.” She wouldn’t be a coward and give in. Not when her decision could affect Melissa. She had to protect her daughter and keep the skeletons of her past in the closet. Locked and sealed.

Her heart thumped against her chest, yet she managed to maintain a steady voice. “I know you want to renovate the Crisis Center. But I can’t help you with this case.” Would her frosty tone put an end to the discussion?

“Dr. Crane! All I ask is that you examine the man and give your report, positive or negative. I have some background information and pictures that Rutherford Senior gave me. Please, take the case.”

“You can give the case to Dr. Anderson, Dr.

Parigio, or Dr. Ameen."

"Emilio Parigio is working on the South American Conference of Mental Illness. He'll be traveling a lot in the next two months. Dr. Ameen is not doing consulting this month with her daughter's wedding coming soon. And Jack Anderson is too green. That leaves—"

"Olivia, on whom you always dump the jobs nobody wants."

"Damn it, Olivia. How can you say that?" He pushed a typed form in front of her. "See this? I just signed your appointment as acting-chairman."

"Oh." Her heart jolted with pride. *Acting-Chairman of Psychiatry at thirty-five.* "Thank you." The title had a nice ring to it. An achievement. Something to strike off her goal list, although it was only a temporary administrative position. Dr. McMillan had chosen her over the other doctors in the department. "I didn't expect. I mean you didn't tell me." For once, she let her exultation warm her voice.

"Congratulations." Luc's voice boomed with pride as if he had received the promotion. "I am sure you will do a great job."

"I'm glad you're happy." Doc sighed with relief. "I was going to announce your appointment at our department meeting. You know I appreciate your hard work. Now, just take the case."

Her delight ruined by Doc's insistence, Olivia laced her fingers together to prevent her hands from shaking. She just couldn't face Jeremy again. The last time she'd seen him she'd looked at him through puffy eyes, her cheek swollen from his blow.

Doc expected her to make an effort to satisfy him. But she couldn't, not for money or title. Not even if he held a knife to her throat. Only Melissa's safety counted.

It was time to remember her psychiatric credo.

Believe in yourself and things will work out. Olivia glanced at the colorful vase adorning a corner of the mahogany desk, and took the deep breath she needed, inhaling the scent of roses, stargazer lilies and early fall flowers.

"I can't." She'd have to give Doc a good reason for him to stop badgering her. "I knew this man years ago. He hurt someone I care about. I wouldn't be objective." She wouldn't add more explanation.

"I see." Doc's brows furrowed in a scowl as he dragged on the words.

"I see," Luc echoed, a suppressed question in his eyes.

What exactly did they see?

She lifted her chin. "There must be someone else to take the case."

"I'd have taken it if I weren't on sabbatical. I'm not supposed to be here. Even if I've showed up every morning for the past two weeks. But that will change as of Monday, now that Luc is here to help you."

"I can handle this case, if you don't mind," Luc said.

Now that was an idea. Maybe she wouldn't have to lose her sleep over the Rutherfords. "Did you renew your medical license?"

"Yes, during one of my trips to the U.S., three years ago. I'll help you with the Rutherford patient. I can sit in during his interviews and help with the diagnosis and treatment. Since I will be leaving in a few months, I would prefer Olivia to cosign the report for follow up."

"Great." Doc stood, not waiting for her response. "You two handle this case together. I trust your competence."

Olivia mentally shrugged, keeping her comments for later. Luc was certainly more than qualified to handle any case *and* sign the report since he'd kept his American license active. She wouldn't waste any more time in useless arguments. "We'll talk about it later."

"Very well. I'm glad this matter is settled."

She turned to leave.

"Olivia," Doc called. "Don't forget this." He scooped up the papers strewn across his desk and tucked them into a folder.

She stared at the Rutherford file, loathe to touch a reminder of her ghastly past.

Doc scowled. "It's part of your responsibilities as acting-chairman."

She grabbed the yellow folder with two fingers as if it were a filthy rag.

Luc extended a hand. "May I have this file? I would like to study the case."

"Be my guest." She handed him the file that burned her heart.

As she raised her head, she met Luc's gaze, simmering with too many questions.

Between Doc's lack of sensitivity for her feelings and Luc's intense curiosity about those same feelings, she'd have a hell of a time maintaining her composure.

Luc held the office door open for her and ushered her into the corridor, his hand on her back, his face too close to her head. "Too many problems? *Ne t'en fais pas, chérie.* Do not worry. I will help you."

"Nothing that I can't handle." Olivia breathed deeply, inhaling his aftershave, and exhaled slowly. Luc George had reappeared in her life four hours ago—the first four hours of the next six months—and he'd already invaded her peaceful space, upset her smooth-running schedule, and interfered in her well-controlled life. He'd have to go away soon. "Luc, about your invitation—"

"Yes?"

She shook her head.

Now that she needed his help to get rid of the Rutherfords, how could she tell him he wasn't welcome?

Chapter Three

Briefly admiring the well-manicured lawn and the neatly trimmed bougainvilleas, Luc sauntered into the McMillan's backyard to join Olivia and bring her a drink while his host took an important phone call.

Olivia's voice chiming from the left led him to a small pond crossed by a wooden bridge that reminded him of a Monet painting. His hands encumbered with two cups, a small bucket of ice, and a bottle of Vermouth, Luc paused at the entrance of the Japanese garden to listen.

Legs crossed under her on a stone bench, Olivia sat barefoot in the shade of a pagoda. Wild lilies, scattered in a palette of orange, yellow and red, permeated the air with a heavy sweet perfume. A picture-perfect setting for a romantic rendezvous. Mesmerized, Luc quickened his pace, all his muscles in a tremor. Finally, he was going to hold her and kiss her.

Her back bent forward, Olivia talked into her cell phone, the late afternoon sun streaking her hair in gold and russet. "Honey, I'll make it up to you. I promise."

Luc froze in place, half-hidden by a maple tree. Who was she talking to?

"Darling, listen to me. I'm very busy right now, but I'll take a day off next week to be with you."

Honey? Darling? The words hit his brain and speared straight toward his heart.

"Melissa, please listen... Wait."

Luc inhaled sharply and exhaled his tension.

Who was Melissa? Whoever she was, Melissa deeply affected Olivia's calm.

Luc frowned as Olivia bolted off the bench. "Mom, don't tell me how to handle my daughter. Put her on again."

Olivia had a daughter?

Ten years was a long period to be alone. But she wasn't wearing a ring. Neither she nor McMillan had mentioned a present husband, fiancé or boyfriend. And she hadn't said a word about this daughter all day long. Still she could have had a child anytime after he'd left. But why had she kept her a secret from him?

He scowled as he trudged through the grass surrounding the pond, his breathing labored, blood pounding against his forehead. "Olivia."

As she turned toward him, she mumbled a quick, "Bye, Mom," and then shoved her cell phone into her purse. "Luc, what are you doing here?" She bent to retrieve her high-heeled shoes from under the stone bench and slipped them on while he dumped the bottle, bucket of ice and glasses on the bench.

"Ah." *Merde.* One of the glasses had shattered on the stone. Mumbling a string of curses, he collected the broken pieces and threw them into the ice bucket.

Why had she not told him she had a daughter?

Something did not make sense here. Olivia Crane had always been a secretive woman, difficult to understand. Still...

Is it possible that Melissa is...?

His jaws tensed. "Olivia, how old is your daughter?"

Lies by omission had cost him a child. Pain spiked through his heart at the thought of his little Paul and the lying bitch, the *salope,* who'd kept his son hidden from him for two years.

Was the nightmare of his past slithering around him again?

Luc resolutely took the last step separating him from Olivia. He wouldn't allow her to knock his structured world out of control the way another woman had, years ago.

"You've been eavesdropping? How dare you?" Her chin lifted, and she scowled.

The memory of a pale toddler still scorched his heart after so many years. He was inflexible when it came to secrets and lies.

"*Dis-moi.* Tell me the truth. How old? Is she mine?" How could she have hidden this from him? She was no better than Brigitte. Were all women fickle liars?

Mon Dieu, not his Olivia. He grabbed her shoulders with more strength than he intended to.

"You're hurting me! Are you crazy?" Slanting green eyes locked with his and widened with disbelief. "Luc, stop it."

Silence drifted over them as they gauged each other's thoughts.

"Did you find out you were pregnant before or after I left?" God help him, he was trembling and shaking her at the same time.

She snorted, a bitter laugh that stunned him. "Melissa is sixteen."

"Sixteen?" He released her and dropped his arms to his side. "Sixteen, but—" His mind blanked. How could it be? Olivia had had a six-year-old when he was here last time? "I don't understand. You have never mentioned a child."

"It's a long story, Luc. I was afraid for her safety. My parents raised her on a farm, in the countryside, hidden from my friends and colleagues who may have asked too many questions." A shadow of panic spread across her face. She hugged herself, her shoulders slumped. "I didn't want anyone to know."

"Even me?" Realization dawned. She had never loved him enough to trust him with her secret. His gut twisted. "Why, Olivia?"

Her eyes brimming with unshed tears, she turned her head and bit her lip.

Was she regretting the long years wasted without love?

"*Chérie*, why did you not confide in me?" He wrapped his arm around her shoulder, but she bristled and averted her eyes.

"Please, let's not talk about it now." She eased out of his hold, her body rigid.

He was missing something. "Who is the father?" Refusing to be jealous of a man who belonged in the past, Luc stepped back and held Olivia at arm's length, his gaze focused on hers.

Her face changed, determination replacing vulnerability. "He's dead."

Luc was a pro at judging people's expression. The hatred in her eyes and tightening of her jaw convinced him she was lying.

"Is that what you told your daughter?"

"In a way, she began the charade. One day she came back from school and asked why she didn't have a daddy like her friends. I started saying her dad was gone. And she said, 'You mean Daddy died in the war like Sue's daddy?' I didn't know what to do. I said yes. She hung onto the story. Later when she asked for more details, I just invented."

"And you let the...confusion drag for years?" Disappointment and understanding warred inside him.

"Yes. Melissa respects and admires the memory of her father." Olivia's lips pursed into a sarcastic line. "A hero who died saving two other soldiers during the Kuwaiti war, before her birth."

"A nice story. But a bad lie." Secrets again.

Secrets that snared his guts in a web of deceit. He cursed himself for not suspecting a deeper problem when she'd ended their relationship. "Olivia, don't you think Melissa is entitled to the truth?"

"The truth is ugly, Luc. Too ugly. I wanted my daughter to grow up happy. Well-adjusted. Respecting the memory of a heroic father, rather than crying about feeling unwanted."

"I assume the father is a *salaud*." He paused searching for the English word. "I mean a...a jerk."

New emotions clashed inside him. Anger against the man responsible for Olivia's fear. Heartache for her hurt. Resentment for the empty years he'd spent trying to forget her with a string of French socialites eager to capture his heart and his newly inherited fortune.

Olivia closed her eyes, pain creased her forehead. Her hands rose, fingers spread as if to fend off a blow. "Please, enough."

"Does he know he has a daughter?" *Be fair*. Jerk or not, a man should not be deprived of his own flesh and blood. Luc would get to the bottom of the story later. Right now he still reeled from her lack of trust in him ten years ago. "Why didn't you tell me about her?"

"I couldn't. You'd have asked too many questions that I wasn't ready to answer. You'd have insisted I tell Melissa the truth and maybe inform her father."

"You know me well." His jaw hardened.

Luc couldn't forgive lies. He'd never forgiven Brigitte for marrying her rich politician without telling Luc she was pregnant with his child. She'd notified him when the toddler, suffering from leukemia, had needed a bone-marrow donor. It had been too late. Luc had met his son on his deathbed.

Dieu merci, Olivia was no Brigitte. She hadn't dumped him to marry for money.

Tears shone in Olivia's eyes, and a soft sob

escaped her. "I've tried so hard to forget the past."

Although he was still nonplussed by her lack of trust, he couldn't resent her for protecting her daughter. Unlike Brigitte, Olivia had suffered for her child's sake.

He ran a soothing hand over her hair, stunned by this new side of Olivia. The strong assertive psychiatrist, the cool woman always in control was now replaced by a mother in distress worrying about her daughter's peace of mind. His sense of protectiveness on alert, he gathered her in his arms.

"Don't cry, please." He waited for her to calm down. She'd braved a lot of problems on her own but collapsed at the mere mention of a threat to her daughter.

"I'm sorry." She sniffled. "I hate to talk about that time in my life."

"I understand." He would have to be patient and tread carefully around her past secrets. Now that her daughter was grown up, Olivia had probably realized it was time to move on with her life, and she'd recommended him for the visiting professor position. What more could he ask for?

He cradled her face between his hands and smiled. "Feeling better?"

She nodded and returned his smile. He studied her features, the wetness of her lashes, the mauve shadows probably due to lack of sleep, and the dimple on her left cheek he used to tickle with the tip of his finger.

His eyes dropped to her luscious lips. Nothing cool or serene here. He watched them quiver as she followed the direction of his gaze. "Olivia, I will help you forget the past."

He bent over her mouth for a quick peck, a soft comforting kiss. His lips fluttered against hers in a gentle caress, then paused. He couldn't draw back. Not now when he was at the gate of paradise. With the slightest pressure, he pulled her closer. Uncontrollable need built inside him.

She, too, seemed to be waiting. He nibbled at the corner of her mouth and tried to ignore the way blood pulsed in his groin. "*Ma chérie.*"

She closed her eyes and leaned into him.

He trailed kisses along her cheek to her forehead. "How I missed you." His chest burned, and his lungs filled with her perfume and the scent of her skin.

"Oh Luc." She raised her head and took a deep breath. The luminescent aqua of her eyes held him enthralled but he wouldn't rush her and risk losing her when he'd just found her again. Whispering French endearments against her hair, he waited for a hint of an invitation.

Years of frustrating loneliness flipped through his mind as he mentally urged her to come to him, to relax in his arms. She clasped her fingers around his nape and he instantly claimed her mouth in a searing kiss, the kiss he'd given her a thousand times in his fantasies. Parting her lips, his tongue explored and played and tasted as he molded her lithe form against him.

How he wanted her. She moaned and clung to his neck, returning his kiss with the same passion that had set him on fire in the past. He was home now, with Olivia in his arms. There was hope for them.

His lips glided along her cheek, and he tucked a strand of hair behind her ear. "I am so glad you invited me. I will protect you and Melissa. Everything will be fine. I will help you get rid of your fears. I promise."

Things would work out, and in time they would inform Melissa of the truth about her father.

For a crazy moment, Olivia tried to believe him, to imagine she could spend the rest of her life in his arms and make up for the time wasted away from him for her daughter's sake. He still wanted her, in spite of the beautiful women who had hung on his arm and probably graced his bed.

Ten years ago, her heart bleeding with concealed love, she'd let him believe she'd never cared enough about him to give up a promising career at UC and follow him to Paris.

If it wasn't for Melissa, she'd have followed him to the end of the earth.

Now Melissa was sixteen, soon to have her own life. Olivia touched her swollen lips, hesitating.

Kiss him. You'll talk later.

But she wouldn't lie now. No matter what it cost, she couldn't let him build dreams based on a lie.

"No, Luc. I didn't invite you." She gazed at the endearing curve of his lips and caressed his cheek, trying to lessen the blow she was about to strike.

"But I received McMillan's letter and your recommendation." His smile slowly faded, and his eyes narrowed.

She sighed, hating herself for the disappointment she'd inflict. Again. "I only evaluated your publications. They were good."

"Olivia, explain yourself." He let go of her, stepped back and crossed his arms. "I am tired of guessing games."

"I knew you as Luc George." She touched his arm. Now that she'd tasted his kisses again, she craved more. He'd been the perfect lover, strong, generous and tender. And so handsome. God, how she longed to be held tightly against the solid length of his muscular body.

"You are digressing." He stared at her, his voice frosty. Conflicting emotions flashed across his face.

"I read several papers written by Dr. Vicour-Michelet. The *Directeur du Centre des Maladies*

Mentales." She dropped her hand and shrugged. It was too late to escape reality. "Luc, I never made the connection. I didn't know your new name."

His eyes held hers, denial darkening their beautiful blue. "But this morning you had my picture on your monitor?"

Tense silence fell between them.

She owed him the truth. "I was checking your website for the first time. I thought Dr. Vicourt-Michelet was an older physician, but I saw your picture and panicked." Her voice came out shaky and strained. "If you weren't already here, I would have stopped you from coming."

There, she'd said it all. And she hated herself.

Luc scanned her face, eyes, mouth, as if he was seeing her for the first time. As if he'd discovered a monster instead of the woman he'd loved.

Her heart twisted. To lose him just when she'd found him again. To lose him twice by her own words and deeds.

"I'm sorry, Luc."

A muscle worked at the base of his throat. "I am the one who is sorry. Such a naïveté on my part is unprecedented. As a renowned psychiatrist, I have miserably failed to understand you."

"Luc, please—"

"Too late." His gaze cold, suddenly intolerant, he raised his hand like a barrier between them. "From now on, our relationship will be strictly professional. I will act the unknown physician you wanted to receive."

He turned and walked toward the house.

Her heart wrenched. Olivia watched him stride over the grass, tall and proud.

Since the moment he'd stepped in her office, she'd wished he'd never come and tried to tell him to go away, but now that she'd tasted his passion, she couldn't conceal her tears. Tears of regret for her wasted life without love. Tears of frustration at the conflict between her heart and her brain. She'd thought herself a strong person, immune to a man's charm. And she had been—until Luc.

With a shaky hand, she dabbed her eyes and her cheeks, and then took a deep breath to collect herself before she joined her hosts.

Melissa, if you only knew how much your mother gave up to protect you.

She'd tried to escape the past, but it had caught up to threaten her present.

****

It was only five in the morning when Luc parked his host's Mercedes in its reserved spot at the CUH parking lot. The night before, the chairman had decided he would spend the day at home packing, and he'd handed Luc a bunch of keys.

The dinner at the McMillans' had tested Luc's endurance. He'd imbibed a whole bottle of wine and engaged his host in a lengthy comparison between the California and the Bourgogne Merlot. Olivia had babbled non-stop with Susan McMillan and swallowed her food in record time before waving good night and walking out.

Luc entered McMillan's office and switched on the lights. He needed to immerse himself in work. His mind still reeled from Olivia's admission that she'd tried to stop his invitation. He'd rehashed their conversation for a good part of the night. To think she'd dated him, slept with him, and appeared to love him, and she'd hidden the fact she had a daughter.

In the past, he'd often noticed her unexplainable silences, when, eyes fixed in the distance, she withdrew into her thoughts. Now he understood her refusal to go out on weekends when she probably visited her parents and daughter. She'd made it up to him during the week and even invited him to her place.

The tiny apartment had surprised him. Bare walls, naked of photos, souvenirs, or any hint of her tastes. The total lack of personality presented an unexpected contrast with the woman he loved. He'd given her a painting of the Eiffel Tower and hung it on her wall. When he questioned her about the austerity of her apartment, she shrugged, claimed she was too busy with her studies and dismissed his doubts with a kiss.

One by one the pieces of the puzzle fell into place.

Mon Dieu, how could he have not guessed she was hiding something?

For a whole year, he'd ignored the niggling warning that something was strange about Olivia's introversion. At the time he'd refused to analyze the woman so dear to his heart, and he'd let love obscure his judgment.

Not anymore, he pledged to himself.

When he had to go back to France because his student visa had expired, Olivia was still doing her residency at UC and was not ready to expatriate herself. For a few years, he'd bombarded her with phone calls and e-mails. He'd thought she would change her mind soon enough.

But she hadn't.

And now? Although he'd kept tabs on her work and achievements, he hadn't seen her for years. She wasn't married, but what if she had another man in her life?

Enfer et damnation! It can't be.

Heat and passion had scorched him as she clung to his neck and molded herself to him. And her kiss had lit a fire in his gut. His groin hardened at the thought she'd wanted him as much as he wanted her.

Had he been too inflexible, too arrogant in his

demand for the truth?

Last night, he'd told her their relationship would be strictly professional. He snorted, knowing there was no way on earth he'd keep such a promise. Even if she hadn't called him back, he would be here for six months, and he planned to put his presence to good use. When he calmed down he'd try to discover the secrets that frightened her, convert her to his faith in truth above all. Until then, he'd have to ignore her and force his body to cooperate.

Now, only work would ease the terrible headache hammering at his temples. Luc opened the Rutherford file, sifted through the papers and started reading, jotting notes on a pad.

Quite an interesting case of antisocial behavior, mental disorders and sexual sadism. He could understand that such a case might repulse a sensitive nature, especially if the violent patient had hurt someone close to her. A relative or a friend? Maybe he'd ask Olivia a few questions. As a doctor, she wouldn't mind helping treat the patient, if only to prevent another drama, would she?

A light knock on the door interrupted his study.

"*Entrez*." He raised his head, surprised by the brightness of the morning sun flooding his office. It was already nine.

The door opened. Olivia walked in, pale but unbending in a navy pantsuit and light blue blouse. He wanted to leap out of his chair, hold her in his arms and ask her to trust him.

A tightening of his muscles reminded him she was off limits, although they would have to work side by side. What had he done to *le bon Dieu* to deserve such a fate? He sucked in a deep breath, inhaling her *Arpège*. The heady fragrance could make a man forget the time of the day.

Luc clenched his fingers. "*Bonjour*."

"Uh-oh." She scanned the office, a frown knitting

her forehead. “Good morning. Where’s Doc?”

“He is not coming today.” Realizing too late his voice sounded gruff, he struggled to be more civilized. “Please, have a seat.”

She glanced at the chair and shook her head. “I have several consultations today. The first one starts in a few minutes.” She pursed her lips as she squinted at the file on his desk, and then she tilted her head. “Would you be interested?”

“Absolutely.” He collected the sheets of paper scattered in front of him.

She pointed at the folder he’d just closed. “What’s this?”

“The Rutherford file. I started studying the case.”

“Oh.” Her lips quivered in disgust.

“We can discuss it whenever you want.”

“I have more urgent cases to handle.” She spun around and walked out.

No need to ask her about Jeremy’s victim now.

He followed her into the hallway leading to the Crisis Center, his gaze locked on the gentle sway of her hips. She seemed to favor severe pantsuits and conservative blouses. He sighed, wishing to see her again in a frilly sundress or sexy shorts. Something more feminine to reveal her shapely legs.

Shaking his head, Luc raised his eyes away from temptation and admired her slender neck and the curls sweeping her shoulders.

Zut alors. If he wanted his body to ignore her, he was taking the wrong approach.

Chapter Four

The young couple waiting for Olivia in the consultation room held each other's hands. Both in their mid-twenties, they exchanged a wary look when she sat at her desk and signaled to Luc to take a chair next to her.

"Good morning. I'm Dr. Crane. We are lucky to have Dr. Luc give a second opinion on your case today." Olivia purposely avoided Luc's long name for fear the nervous couple might run out of the door.

She scanned their medical records and frowned, slowing down while she focused on the answers they'd filed.

Incredible. Of all the mental disorders she usually faced, her first joint patients with Luc had to suffer from sexual disorders. Cripes, why couldn't they have a normal depression or a healthy schizophrenia?

Not to worry. She'd handled worse situations. She held out the sheets to Luc. "Peter and Carla have already had a physical and a full battery of tests. They were referred to our Crisis Center by their respective doctors."

"Good," said Luc as he shuffled through the papers.

Olivia crossed her hands on her desk and faced the three-hundred pound male patient. "Peter, can you describe the symptoms you experienced the last time you had intercourse?"

The heavy man shifted in his chair. "Carla and I have been living together for the past two months, and—"

"And for the last two months he hasn't been able to keep it up after he enters me," the skinny Carla blurted out.

Embarrassed, Peter nodded, lowered his head, and mumbled, "I don't know why. I want to make love to Carla. And I'm aroused. But then I lose it and can't stay inside. Last time Carla got mad and punched me in the chest."

"And you didn't touch me for a week." Carla threw a nasty look at her companion. "If a man loves a woman, he's supposed to show it with kisses and caresses." She turned to Olivia. "Right, doctor?"

Olivia felt Luc's heavy gaze on her. She could swear he wanted to agree with the woman but was too professional to make a comment now. After the fiasco of last night's confrontation, Olivia wouldn't let him lay a finger on her.

She resolutely turned toward her patient. "I understand how you feel, Carla, but Peter has a medical problem. We can help him."

Peter's shoulders caved in. "Carla, how do you expect me to touch you when you yell so much?" His voice was surprisingly weak for such a bulky man.

"What is the point of getting married if you won't touch me?"

"Please." Olivia tapped on her desk. "I don't think you are ready to get married yet. Are you taking any medication, Peter?"

"No, doctor."

"He should take Viagra." Carla snorted, then shot a glance at Olivia. "Hey, doctor, can you give him some Viagra?"

"First, I'm going to refer you to a sex therapy clinic to help with the erectile disorder." She jotted a few notes on her pad then turned toward Luc. "Dr. Luc, what's your opinion?"

"I concur with Dr. Crane's decision. The tests indicate we can eliminate diabetic neuropathy and any organic causes. The Masters and Johnson's sensate focus exercises will help you explore ways of giving physical pleasure to each other without the psychological demands of demonstrating sexual competence."

"You mean he'll be able to give me pleasure without an erection?"

"Yes, Carla," Luc said, while glancing at Olivia. "When a man really loves a woman, he can give her unforgettable pleasure."

Olivia forgot her patients as her eyes widened on Luc. There was such heat in his gaze she swallowed, her fingers clenching around her pen.

"But what about my hard—my erection?" With an anguished frown, Peter crossed his hands on his belly, protecting his groin.

"Hopefully, it will come in time. The Masters and Johnson's is an excellent method." Luc reassured him with a smile.

Eager to end the awkward moment, Olivia scribbled a couple of prescriptions and gave them to Peter. "Now I want you both to relax. You'll be fine if you follow the treatment they'll give you at the sex therapy clinic. They'll send me a report after each session. I'll see you both in a month." She accompanied them to the door and then resumed her place behind the desk.

"Poor guy. It is terrible to love a woman and not be able to keep her in onc's arms," said Luc as Olivia collected her papers and closed the medical report.

Olivia read accusation in the tone of his voice and the piercing look he shot her. Refusing to be intimidated, she leveled a sharp gaze at him. If he was looking for a squabble, she was ready to fight back. "I wouldn't know." She shrugged and tilted her head. "Never personally met a man with this kind of problem."

"And how many men are we talking about?"

Luc's jaw hardened. He crossed his arms over his chest.

"What's the matter with you? Your questions are totally uncalled for." She didn't like his inquisitive tone, but her stomach tightened with unexpected hope. Was he jealous?

"Are you dating someone, Olivia?" A deep scowl creased his forehead as he leaned forward, elbows propped on the armrests, fingers tented.

"Hey, enough." Oh God, could he still care about her? Even after she'd admitted not asking him to come back?

Her traitorous heart somersaulted. She'd walk into his arms without hesitation. But on her terms. No questions asked. Her past forgotten, erased.

"You read all my papers before writing your recommendation, Dr. Crane. Now, I am documenting you, my new colleague. Fair enough." His voice rang, metallic and controlled. "Tell me."

Documenting her? Of all the nerve.

"Dr. Vicour-Michelet, may I remind you that you are here on business. You have no right to interfere in my personal life." A surge of unexpected anger flooded through her, and she banged her fist on the desk.

Why did he demand more than she was willing to give? Why did he expect her to adhere to his sacrosanct mission of truth above feelings?

To think that for a minute she'd imagined he wanted her back, even after she told him the truth about his invitation. Talk about being delusional.

"What personal life, Olivia?" He held her arm, his gaze capturing hers with male authority.

Lips pursed, she thrust backward against her chair. "How dare you?"

"Have you already forgotten how you responded to my kiss last night?"

Luc's questions slapped her with the strength of

a hurricane. The blood drained from her face as she bolted from her chair and pointed to the door. "Get out of here."

Silence hovered over them for a moment.

"I am sorry, Olivia. I did not mean to upset you. I know I can help you overcome your problems if you just let me." He raked his hair, his gaze burning her with its intensity, but she was beyond listening.

"Go back to Paris, Luc." She hissed between gritted teeth. "Go back and stay there. I don't need your help. I have a beautiful daughter and a successful career. My schedule and my life are proceeding exactly as I've planned them."

"Fine." He raised both hands in a conciliatory gesture. "But I am stunned by this situation. Help me understand you. We dated for a year. I loved you. Why did you not trust me?"

Loved. He used the past tense. Even if his love had survived for ten years, she'd killed it with her confession. The sadness underlying his question went straight to her heart. She dropped back into her chair, rubbing her forehead to lessen the tension.

Why did he have to linger over the painful past?

Luc touched her hand and enfolded it in his large one. "Olivia, you are a psychiatrist. You know you can't bury your past forever. Not when you have a teenage daughter. At some point, you will have to deal with it. Can you please tell me why you hid your daughter from me?"

"Why can't you understand?" She snatched her hand from his and exhaled, wishing she had a magic formula to erase her bitter past. "When I was a student, I was still hiding her from everybody at med school." Resting her head against the back of the chair, she closed her eyes. "I told you I was terrified for her safety. Melissa is unfortunately the mirror image of her father. I was afraid that he'd find out he has a daughter and hurt us both."

"Did he ever threaten you?"

Olivia blinked and struggled to suppress her bitterness. *Threaten* was putting it mildly. "He told me to 'get rid of it' when I said I was pregnant. And he got upset when I protested."

"How upset?" Luc punched the palm of his left hand with his fist.

Feeling her control slipping under his scrutiny, she turned her head.

"Did he hit you?"

She didn't answer. But he must have read the humiliating truth in her eyes.

"*Mon Dieu*. I wish I had known. I would have killed this monster. Is that the reason you turned away from me?"

She bit her lip, loathe to tell him how much she'd cried after he left. "Listen, we dated on and off during that year, but you were going back to France, and I wanted to concentrate on my career. Why would we start a long-distance relationship? Besides, I couldn't trust anyone. Any man after..." Shaking her head, she averted her gaze. Luc was far too perceptive. "I was too frightened."

"And you still are. You sacrificed a lot because of your inner fear. Don't you think you need help, Dr. Crane? You need to learn to trust people again."

"I'm fine now. When Melissa started high school, I introduced her to my boss and colleagues. I'm very proud of her." She stood to signify the end of this conversation that had drained her.

Damn it. She didn't need a shrink. After sampling his kisses last night, she roused to a surprising reality. She wanted him again. She wanted her French lover who lavished her with pleasure and tenderness during steamy nights.

His eyes narrowed, Luc crossed his arms over his chest. "But you still have not told your daughter the truth." The archetypal psychiatrist, he followed the same line of questions.

Irritation flickered through her, and she struggled not to shout at him. “That’s not your problem.” The minute she’d confided in him, he tried to impose his views. “You see why I couldn’t tell you my secret? I didn’t want anyone interfering and destroying my daughter’s peace of mind.”

Poor Melissa. She was doing a fine job destroying her own peace of mind with her sudden inappropriate curiosity. Olivia hadn’t slept much in the last month, more precisely since the day in hell when Melissa had asked to see a picture of her father. Olivia had struggled to deal with her daughter’s request without hurting her, but hadn’t come up with a solution yet.

“She’s entitled to a respectful memory of her father.” Now Jeremy’s presence in Cincinnati added more fuel to her motherly fears. Olivia’s skin prickled. Any indiscretion could seriously jeopardize her daughter’s happiness.

Luc’s gaze sharpened. “Her respectful memory is a lie. You should tell your daughter before she finds out on her own.” He touched her arm gently. “Olivia, remember I told you I went through something similar—but from the other side—and lost my son. It will always hurt.” The little lines around his eyes crinkled at the painful memory. “Would you not advise your patients to face the truth and deal with it?”

Darn, but he’d ruffled her feathers with his patronizing tone. Olivia felt like screaming in frustration. *Unbelievable.* She had become a patient for him. An interesting patient he was determined to cure. And on top of that, he questioned her professional competence.

“Do you think I don’t realize this?” She eyed him with acerbity. Why couldn’t he see things her way? “I’ve spent years pondering this problem. To tell

Melissa about her father or not. I know she'll be hurt if the truth gets out." Olivia shook her head, trying to fight the panic that clutched her throat. "I don't want her to suffer. What kind of mother would intentionally harm her daughter?"

"A loving mother who wants to teach her daughter the right values, as you certainly do."

She didn't like the harshness in his voice and the one-way direction of his thoughts. Deliberately ignoring his frown, Olivia squared her shoulders and lifted her chin. She would stick to the decision she made before Luc's arrival.

"Melissa is still too young. I plan to tell her about her father when she's twenty-five. By then she'll be mature enough to understand." Olivia quashed the impulse to grit her teeth. "Now, are you done with this psychoanalysis?"

He stared at her hard. "Yes, for the time being."

Her pager buzzed. *Saved by the bell.* She sighed in relief and dialed the number.

"An attempted suicide." She scowled at him as she yanked on her white jacket. Had she been wrong to protect Melissa and grant her a picture-perfect father?

Damn you, Luc, for unleashing old memories and throwing doubt in my mind.

Chapter Five

Luc stood at the door of the emergency unit, adjusting the collar of the white coat he'd grabbed from a closet in the hallway. Olivia's suffering at a young age gnawed at his gut. She hadn't revealed the name of Melissa's father, but he hadn't wanted to push her too hard. Eventually, he would find out. Right now, they had a patient who needed their full attention.

"Can you talk to me, Hailey?" Olivia held the hand of the young woman whose stomach had been pumped.

The patient wept as she rubbed her belly.

"Your stomach hurts? Are you in pain?"

"It's not my stomach. It's my baby." Big tears rolled down the young woman's cheeks.

"Are you pregnant?" Olivia touched Hailey's flat abdomen.

Luc flipped through the patient's chart. "There's nothing here about her being pregnant."

"Hailey, did you lose a baby?" Olivia asked in a soft voice. The patient contorted, her body wracked by uncontrollable sobs. "Tell us what happened. We're here to help you," Olivia said with the same gentle tone.

Finally, the crying subsided. Hailey hiccupped. "Nobody can help me. My baby is gone."

"How?"

"I had an abortion. My boyfriend didn't want a child. He already has three by his ex. He said 'later.' When he finds a job. I told him I wanted my baby, but he took me to that doctor." Hailey punched at her chest as her voice rose. “And I let him do it. I let them kill my baby.”

“When did that happen?” Luc asked as he recorded the information. A classic case of unwanted pregnancy followed by abortion, guilt, depression and attempted suicide.

“Two months ago. I cried day and night. My boyfriend left me. I feel so guilty.” The woman covered her eyes and started crying again. “I want to die. I took all the tranquilizers the doctor gave me.”

“How do you feel now, Hailey? Do you still want to die?”

“No, but I have nothing to live for.”

“Yes, you do. You’re young, healthy and beautiful,” Olivia said with a soothing smile that reached deep into his heart. She, too, was young, healthy and beautiful, and content with what she had. But was she really happy?

“Did you ever work?” Olivia asked her patient. Although she remained calm and composed, he was sure she would go to extra lengths to help this patient.

“I was working as a waitress at night. Had to pay for my schooling before I got pregnant. I wanted to be a nurse.”

“I’m going to have a social worker take care of you. Eventually, you should go back to school and stand on your own two feet.”

“What for? My baby’s gone.”

“You’re young. You can still become a nurse. You’ll be able to help a lot of people. With time you will become independent and strong.” Her voice low but firm, Olivia squeezed the patient’s shoulder as if she wanted to infuse her with her own strength.

Luc stopped writing as he studied Olivia’s determined expression, her narrowed eyes and pursed lips. Independent and strong. She preached what she practiced.

How could he explain to her there was more to life than her empty philosophy? She had been emotionally wounded, a deep wound that he hadn't been able to guess at and heal ten years ago. She'd put her happiness on hold and lived a lonely life. How could he convince her they belonged together?

As for him... He snorted. He'd tried hard to forget her. To no avail. She had to stop walking away from him, her chin raised, when he wanted her forever at his side.

Hailey sniffled and rubbed the back of her hand over her red-rimmed eyes. "I wish I could be independent. I hate men. They're all jerks."

Luc stepped forward. "All men are not bad, Hailey. One day you will meet a good man who will really love you. And when you do, keep him, because men like that are not easy to replace. Correct, Dr. Crane?"

Correct or not, Dr. Crane fiddled with the pager clipped on her belt, ready to hurl it at his head as she glared at him. "Dr Luc, do you mind waiting outside? I'll continue alone here."

He stifled a smile of satisfaction. Olivia's angry reaction was a proof that his words had penetrated her cold façade.

"I will see you later, Hailey. Do not worry, you may have many children one day. This bad experience should not mark your life for ever." He leveled a pointed look at Olivia. "With the correct therapy, you will eventually put it behind you and learn to move on." *This one is for you, Dr. Crane.* They were both psychiatrists, but definitely had a different view of the same problem.

Olivia spun around, giving him her back. "Hailey, I'll have you admitted into the psych unit for a few days, and then you'll join a therapy group at the Crisis Center. You don't need any medicines now," Olivia said as Luc walked out.

Had he pushed her beyond the limit of her patience? Would his words continue to buzz in her ears and remind her he was here, ready to hold her and help her?

****

To distract himself from Olivia's problem—his problem too—Luc settled at McMillan's desk and opened the Rutherford file. He took out the pictures and studied them. The man was good-looking, neat and presentable, with an interesting cleft in the chin *à la Michael Douglas*. On thorough examination, Luc thought the patient's head tilted in an I-am-above-the-law arrogance and the smile extended into a cruel line.

After reading psychiatric references that could help in the Rutherford case for half an hour, Luc shut the book and glanced at his watch. He should go back and soothe Olivia. He had riled her enough with his direct questions and thinly veiled comments. Leaving a breach in their professional relationship was not advisable. He'd be wise to avoid questioning her for a couple of days until she calmed down.

He knocked on her door and entered her office, ready to appease her with a charming smile. "Olivia—"

He stopped dead in his tracks.

A teenage girl sat in Olivia's leather chair, a cell phone clamped to her ear, her feet crossed on top of the desk. She stood immediately with an "I'll call you back" and shut her phone, staring at him with obvious curiosity.

"Hi, I'm Melissa Crane."

"*Bonjour*, I am Dr. Luc, a colleague of your mother."

"Oh, the visiting French doctor." A smile spread over her face. "She told us about you. Having fun in Cincinnati?"

"Very much. Especially at this time of the year. The foliage is gorgeous." Luc scanned the tall girl, a delightful teenager with pale blue eyes, full lips and a blond mane cascading over her shoulders and back.

"I'm waiting for Mom. She didn't come home last night for dinner, so I decided to surprise her today." Melissa turned her head toward the door.

Luc studied her perky profile, the high cheeks bones, and the slight upturn of her delicate nose. He stifled the nagging feeling of déjà-vu. Of course, it was normal that Olivia's daughter looked familiar, in spite of her different features and fair coloring.

She faced him again, her light blue eyes glittering like stardust. "I'm taking my mom to lunch."

"That is a good idea, *Mademoiselle*. I am sure your *maman* will be delighted to see you."

"*Mademoiselle*?" She giggled. "I like that. Everyone around here treats me like a kid. Especially Mom."

While mother and daughter entertained each other, he'd finish reading the Rutherford case. His thoughts flew to the file he'd left on McMillan's desk and the pictures of the blond patient.

The blond patient?

His gaze flipped back to Melissa, his mind drawing a jittery parallel between the features of Jeremy Rutherford and the teenager standing in front of him.

Same light blue eyes, same profile, and same wide lips. And the same sandy colored hair. Even the little dimples in the round cheeks and delicate chin. Olivia had mentioned Melissa was the mirror image of her father.

I knew this man years ago.

Olivia's words played back in his brain and pounded with a new meaning.

He hurt someone I care about. I won't be objective.

Luc didn't doubt for a second that the woman Jeremy had hurt was Olivia herself.

The psychotic patient was Melissa's father?

Mon Dieu, mon Dieu! Jeremy Rutherford. Could it be possible?

His jaws clenched, Luc leaned against the doorframe and frowned, putting in place the missing piece of the puzzle. A muscle jerked at the base of his throat as he studied Melissa's features.

It all made sense. Olivia's refusal to deal with the Rutherford case. The secrets she staked deep in her heart. Her fear for her daughter.

For years, she'd sacrificed her happiness to avoid any contact with Jeremy and now the devil from her past had come to haunt her.

Conflict of interest. A huge one.

"Dr. Luc, what's wrong? Are you sick?"

Melissa's voice sounded exactly like her mother's.

"A slight headache."

He wasn't lying. Blood thumped against his temples, and his mind swirled with confusing thoughts. He had to sort through Olivia's many secrets and organize his approach to the Rutherford case.

How would he remain impartial while evaluating this patient? The man who had abused Olivia and tried to force her to abort her baby. The same man who'd indirectly caused her to mistrust all men and reject Luc's love.

Enfer et damnation. Would he be able to refrain from shoving his fist in this monster's face the minute he walked in for his consultation? But Luc had no choice. In view of the new information, he couldn't let Olivia deal with this case.

He studied Melissa's features one last time and

straightened to leave. "If you will excuse me, *Mademoiselle* Melissa, I have some work to do." She smiled when he used that title.

"Oh, you're leaving? I wanted to ask you questions about Paris. I hope to visit France in a year or two."

His heart went out to the girl who'd grown up without a father. He'd have lavished her with love. God only knew how badly he wanted a child.

If only Olivia had trusted him.

His jaw tightened so much it hurt. "I am sure you will come here another time for lunch. We can talk then."

Would Olivia allow him a friendship with her daughter? After his questioning that morning, his relationship with Olivia teetered on a brink, but in spite of her bravado, she needed his protection. And she was going to receive it, even reluctantly.

"It's not easy to come all the way here. I just got my driver's license a month ago, and Mom doesn't let me drive that far."

"How did you come?"

"Tony drove me."

"Tony?"

"Dr. Tony Burk. Mom's friend. He came for dinner last night and stayed overnight. He took me with him on his way to work."

Mom's friend? Overnight? Luc's breath clogged in his chest as the three words sucker punched him.

Was there no end to Olivia's secrets?

****

Olivia froze in the doorway, unable to take another step. Her daughter was chatting with Luc. In her office.

"Melissa? What are you doing here?"

"Hi Mom. Missed you." Melissa jumped from her chair and came forward. Throwing her arms around Olivia's neck in a big hug, the teenager chuckled.

"Dr. Luc and I have been killing time talking."

Olivia hugged her back. Oh Lord, what had Melissa been discussing with Luc? He stood, handsome and somber, arms crossed over his chest. His blue gaze, fixed on Olivia, darkened by the second. She owed him no explanation, certainly not after the way he'd grilled her this morning.

Ignoring him, she smiled at Melissa. "Honey, I didn't expect to find you here."

"I know. I'm inviting you for a surprise lunch at the Rotating Tower."

"It's a surprise, all right. You're not supposed to drive such a long distance on your own."

"I didn't. Honest, Mom. Tony drove me."

"Oh." With Luc constantly around in the past two days, Olivia had forgotten about Tony, but she'd bet a month's salary that Luc's scowl had something to do with the mention of her friend's name. She sighed, her skin prickling with a premonition. Since Luc's arrival, the tidy strings of her life had tangled beyond belief.

"I was upset when you didn't show up last night for dinner." Her daughter was not one to mince words when she felt justified. "Nana suggested I go and see you. Tony stayed overnight and brought me with him."

Oh dear. Why couldn't Melissa skip the awkward details?

Luc's forehead wrinkled into a mesh of tempestuous lines. Not that Olivia's private life was any of his business, but knowing Luc's professional tendency to dig into everyone's thoughts, he would launch into a series of new questions at the first opportunity—annoying questions about her relationship with Tony.

Tension balled between her shoulders, but her body yearned for Luc's unforgettable caress. Why would she have to argue with him when she'd rather be kissing him?

"Melissa, I—"

"Don't tell me you're too busy again. Please, Mom." Melissa's voice wheedled.

Melissa had gone out of her way to spend time with her. Olivia's heart melted. "Of course, I can come." A mother-daughter lunch would please her immensely.

"If you'll excuse me, I'll leave you to your lunch," Luc said, taking heed of her crystal clear message.

Before Olivia could breathe a sigh of relief, Melissa spun toward him. "Dr. Luc, can you come with us? I'd love to hear stories about France."

"I don't want to intrude. You are trying to have a private time with your *maman*."

Melissa scoffed. "Not private, just a fun time. You and Mom and me. Tony's coming too. Please, Dr. Luc," she insisted in a cajoling tone that won her an amused smile from Luc.

"Shame on me to ever disappoint you, *Mademoiselle* Melissa." The smart man danced to the tune Melissa played, a sure way to win her favors. Upon Melissa's insistence—and probably her mention of Tony—Luc plopped down into a chair. His frown hadn't relaxed a single line, but he didn't seem eager to leave now.

Olivia sighed, hating the irritating ideas of her headstrong daughter. Hopefully, Tony would be detained in a therapy session. But before Olivia had time to formulate an answer, she heard a light knock.

Tony walked in, a bright smile on his face, and swept Olivia into a bear hug. "Where has my favorite shrink been hiding? I need to have a talk with McMillan. That old tyrant is going to kill you on the job."

Olivia peeked around Tony's burly shoulders at Luc's arched brow and braced herself, waiting for

Tony to turn and notice their foreign guest. "Come on, Tony. You're busier than I am."

"Sweetheart, I know where to draw the line. You shouldn't have dumped us for the French expert last night. We'll see enough of him in the next six months."

Count on Tony to step in it. Luc hadn't moved from his chair, but a sarcastic smile stretched his lips.

"Tony, may I introduce Dr. Lucien de Vicour-Michelet? Luc for short," Olivia said without a smile.

Tony spun around, scanned Luc and burst out laughing. "Talk about a blunder."

Luc took his own sweet time to stand up while Olivia finished the introduction. "This diplomatic man is Dr. Tony Burke, famous psychologist and reputed the world over for his refined language."

She exhaled, wondering how this scene would end. But she was dealing with two pros.

Tony extended his hand. "Luc, so happy to finally meet you. I must say I've heard a lot about you," he added with a wink while shaking Luc's hand.

"I must say I have not heard a thing about you." Luc continued to pump on Tony's hand with the same force. "*Enchanté.* A great surprise for me. Absolute surprise. Olivia as you know is a very busy person. She has not found the time to mention your name yet. A simple oversight, *n'est-ce pas, ma chère*?"

Ignoring Luc's half-smile, Olivia rolled her eyes and shrugged. "Yes." They were about to dislodge each other's radial bones with their shaking.

"Let's go to lunch," Melissa chimed in. "This is going to be fun. Too bad Nana's not with us. She'd have enjoyed this outing."

Olivia almost choked. As if she needed her mother to bless her choice of boyfriends, past or fake, and nudge her into choosing one for happily ever after. Just the type of fun Olivia needed.

She had often imagined lunch with Luc—breakfast and dinner too—but she'd never thought she'd be driving to a restaurant with her ex-lover sitting in the back of her van next to her dear friend Tony.

In the front seat, Melissa chatted about school, her friends and the coming prom, with Tony giving know-it-all advice on every subject just like a stepfather. Olivia caught Luc's somber scowl in the rearview mirror and the disgruntled look he threw at Tony. Luc's mood seemed to have plummeted to an all-time low.

A fun lunch indeed.

"We're at the Rotating Tower," Olivia announced. She slipped from the van before Luc could climb out and extend a helping hand. Raising her head, she scanned the tall building. "There's a gorgeous view from up there, and they make the best ribs."

Luc crossed his arms. "Is this all you remember about the Rotating Tower?"

She stiffened, not ready to elaborate or dwell on happy memories. Luc had brought her here for dinner once. The night he told her he loved her and later stayed at her place for a memorable night. Her cheeks flamed as she opened her mouth and then closed it without a sound.

"I remember our dinner here," Luc whispered against her hair. "And the after-dinner drink, of course. Do you?"

She glared at him, hoping Melissa and Tony hadn't heard Luc's reminiscence. Her lips pursed, she spun around, gave her key to the valet and led the way to the elevator and the rotating restaurant on the thirtieth floor.

When they reached the table, Luc sat next to her

before Tony could appropriate the place. Melissa slid into the chair across from Luc, and Tony settled beside her daughter.

"We better order right away. I have patients this afternoon." Olivia signaled to the waitress, and they placed their orders.

"Look how beautiful it is." Melissa waved at the scenic view beyond the glass panels surrounding the restaurant.

"Gorgeous view," Tony commented as he reached for the soft drink the waitress placed in front of him.

After a quick glance at the panoramic sight of high-rises, beyond the Ohio River, Luc shifted in his seat and faced Olivia. His broody expression melted into a flicker of a smile. "Exceptional." She blinked at the double entendre. "Breathtaking," he murmured as their gazes collided.

Her cheeks burned. She fluttered her napkin with a swift gesture and smoothed it on her lap. Somehow, she preferred his previous gloominess to this confident teasing.

Stop it, Luc.

Chapter Six

What had caused Luc's change of mood? Had he decided to stop dwelling on the past? Or maybe he'd realized that Tony wasn't a dangerous rival?

Olivia squinted at him. His grin widened as if he seemed amused by her unspoken questions.

She snorted inwardly. Rival to what? Luc had just arrived in Cincinnati two days ago, after a long absence. How could such an attractive man still be unattached?

Maybe he enjoyed his freedom too much and the fringe benefits attached to let any woman capture his heart. But he'd always been a possessive man, fiercely protective of what he considered his. Did he still think of her as exclusively his? *Nonsense.*

The waitress brought their orders. Hardly noticing the aroma of garlic and herbs emanating from her plate, Olivia speared her steak, still puzzled by Luc's sudden change of attitude.

"Mom?" Her daughter's voice cut through her reverie. "Mom?"

"Huh?"

"I said, 'Have you found the picture?'"

Olivia's heart flipped over at her daughter's aggressive tone. "The picture?"

"My dad's picture. I asked you a month ago to get me one. Don't tell me you forgot again?"

"Huh? No, I didn't forget." Olivia wrinkled the napkin on her lap with an icy hand. Of course, she hadn't forgotten. Actually, she'd spent several nights awake, debating how to tackle this new problem.

For sixteen years Melissa had lived happy,

content with the stories Olivia invented to answer her innocent questions. Why the sudden need to see a picture of her damned father?

"Mom, I've never seen a single picture of him." Melissa's voice wobbled with indignation and then firmed as she addressed Luc. "My dad died a war hero. There should be a way to find an old photo of him."

A war hero. Olivia stifled a snort. It was almost blasphemy to refer to Jeremy Rutherford as war hero. He was a jerk of the worst type, a womanizer and an abuser. Olivia bit her lip hard. A vicious pain stabbed her insides, but she couldn't crush her daughter's heart with the truth.

"Honey, he's been gone too long." Olivia scratched the back of her neck to calm an itch and wished she could scratch Jeremy out of her past as easily. For all she knew, the sleazeball might be having fun with a string of girlfriends at this moment. Unless he was already in jail.

"You said he was your first love. Don't you miss him, Mom?"

Olivia threw a glance at Luc and prayed for patience. "Yes, he was my first love." *And the curse of my life*. "But, he's been gone for a long time. We can't live in the past. Darling, you are the most important person for me now. I want you to promise you'll forget the sad thoughts and be happy with all the blessings we have."

"Yes, Mom."

Her daughter's dutiful tone didn't fool her. Olivia knew there would be a follow-up. For the time being, she'd evaded a huge pothole.

"Tell me more about your plans to visit France, *Mademoiselle* Melissa." A paternal smile at the teenager softened Luc's firm tone of voice.

"For heaven's sake Luc, drop the *Mademoiselle*. She's only sixteen." Olivia huffed.

"A very mature sixteen I must say. I tell you what, Melissa, we will both use each other's first names." A delighted smile brightened the girl's face. Luc ignored Olivia's exasperated sigh and Tony's interested gaze. "Now about your trip. Have you seriously discussed it with your *maman*?"

"We talked about it. Mom knows I want to go." Melissa tilted her chin up in a show of independence.

Luc shot a quick look at Olivia as if he too noticed her daughter could be a handful in spite of her apparent sweetness. "How long would you like to spend there?"

"Ten months. My sophomore year. I have a friend whose mother is French. We'll be staying in Paris together, but I plan to visit Normandy where the Americans landed during World War II. And I want to take a side trip to Kuwait."

"What?" Olivia squealed as Tony's exclamation echoed Luc's. Under the table, her foot hit Luc's outstretched leg in a jerky movement. "Sorry, Luc," she said automatically without looking at him. "Why Kuwait?" Her eyes froze open, and her heart sank to her toes.

"I want to see the place where my dad died. Mom, I didn't talk to you about it, because you always change the subject when I mention him."

"Honey, it's not that easy to go to these countries." Olivia clenched her knife, her knuckles whitening, as she flicked a glance from Melissa to Tony.

A deep scowl replaced Tony's cheerful expression. The psychologist definitely knew about Melissa's parentage and shared Olivia's anxiety. How long had she entrusted Tony with her secret?

Luc smothered the bitterness that pervaded his spirit whenever he was faced with secrets. If the tightness of her jaw was any indication, Olivia needed all the sympathy and support he could give her.

Melissa patted her mother's hand. "Don't worry, Mom, I won't go alone. I learned from a friend that the Department of Defense organizes tours for veterans' families. I'm a vet's child. I'm sending them a letter to inquire about their war hero, Joe Madden, and if they still have a picture of him."

"You're writing to the DOD?" Olivia croaked. The color drained from her face. Panic flashed in her widened eyes. For a second, Luc feared she might collapse. Tony, as pale as Olivia, fiddled with a bag of sugar without opening it, a nervous tic playing at the corner of his left eye.

"What's the matter, Mom? I just want a picture of my father. That's all. Mom?" Melissa leaned forward and squeezed her mother's fingers. "Relax. Look at your face. It's not like I'm committing a crime, for heaven's sake." Melissa shrugged and turned toward Luc. "I was born after my father's death. My parents never had the chance to get married. Mom doesn't even have a picture of her fiancé."

"The whole situation is too sad for you and your *maman*."

Luc caught the rapid blinking of Olivia's eyelids. Strong, independent and tough Olivia, reduced to that shivering state by her daughter. He wanted to take away the pain that creased tell-tale lines under her eyes. He swallowed the rest of his wine and then dabbed his mouth with his napkin while he formulated a quick plan of action. If he couldn't comfort Olivia, he would at least try to help.

"Melissa, how would you like to come and spend next summer in France? Your sophomore year is in three years. Why wait so long?" He purposely shifted the conversation back to the French trip. "I can arrange for you to stay in Paris with friends who have a daughter your age. And then you can visit with my mother at our family *château* in Bourgogne."

"Oh my God, you have a chateau?"

"Not a huge one, but big enough. My mother will be delighted to take you around."

"I'd love to go. Mom?"

"I don't mind, if it's not too much trouble for Luc to organize your summer." Olivia sent him a grateful look. "But forget about that Kuwait trip. And asking for information and pictures from the DOD. We don't need sad reminders."

"But, Mother—"

"Melissa, do not make your *maman* cry," Luc said with gentle firmness, determined to erase the shadow from Olivia's aqua eyes. "You are going to promise that you will forget all about Kuwait, the DOD, and the past. I will bring you pamphlets about France in a few days and together we will plan a fabulous vacation for you. *D'accord?*"

A silence hovered around the table. Melissa's gaze rested on her mother's face, and then she nodded. "Deal."

"Your promise, please," Luc said, praying he'd managed to influence the girl. He mentally ticked the seconds while Melissa hesitated. Dreams glittered in her eyes as she peered at the window panels and the scenery unfolding beyond.

Finally, she inhaled deeply. "I won't send the letter if it hurts my mother so much."

Olivia sighed and squeezed her daughter's hand. "Thank you, darling."

"Right decision, Melissa," Luc said, pleased to see Olivia relax. He immediately launched into a description of the castles in the *Vallée de la Loire*. A hint of a smile curled Olivia's lips as she listened with obvious relief to Luc's anecdotes and her daughter's questions.

But Tony's nervousness puzzled Luc. The

psychologist forked his steak, hardly eating. He rolled his bread into little balls and dropped them on his plate. Was it worry about Olivia and her daughter that caused Tony's visible tension? Or jealousy toward an unexpected rival?

The waitress wheeled a cart with mouthwatering desserts near their table.

"Hmm, French *gateaux*." Olivia licked her lips.

"A chocolate *mille-feuilles*, maybe?" Luc asked, delighted to see her mind off the blistering subject.

She shot him a surprised look.

As if he could ever forget their midnight strolls to the all-night bakery. A coffee and one of those scrumptious *mille-feuilles* gave Olivia a study break before the board exams. Of course, Luc always looked for a reason to be with her.

"Yes, I love Napoleons."

"I will have the same," he told the waitress exactly as he used to say ten years ago. *Same pastry, same woman.* Luc turned his head toward her and gave her a rapid wink. "I am faithful to my tastes." Olivia's smile brightened her lovely features.

"I see." Her lips puckered as if she tried to suppress an urge to chuckle. He could swear she'd followed the train of his thoughts and engaged in a secret conversation with him while their two companions were busy choosing their desserts.

"Are you?" He clasped the hand she had dropped in her lap. "Faithful too?" he whispered as he leaned toward her and picked up the napkin that had slid to the floor.

"Luc!" Her gaze flicked from his face to her daughter and Tony.

He took a bite of his *mille-feuilles* and savored the creamy taste, his eyes fixed on hers. "*Delicieux.* As I knew it would be." He licked his lips and squeezed her hand under the table. Her eyes rounded at his suggestive motion. She was adorable, all rattled up, her cheeks reddening by the second. If only he could get rid of Tony and the teenager.

“Don’t worry about Jeremy,” he whispered to appease her anxiety.

A gasp escaped her, and her jaw fell.

Melissa had finally pointed to a fruit torte. Luc released Olivia’s hand. “How about you, Tony? What are you having?”

“Tony doesn’t eat sweets,” Olivia said as she motioned the waitress to take the cart away.

“I’m diabetic.” Tony shook his head sadly. “Olivia always reminds me of my diet.”

Luc frowned, certainly not expecting Tony to be a sick man and Olivia to play the caring friend. What kind of relationship was that?

Granted the psychologist was nice, cheerful, attentive to Olivia’s needs, affectionate to Melissa, but he simply wasn’t Olivia’s type. Too big, too loud, too...wrong. Except for the chaste kiss Tony had placed on Olivia’s cheek, he hadn’t struck Luc as a besotted lover. Luc was tempted to stop worrying about Tony as a rival.

When they finished their lunches and walked toward the exit, Melissa touched his arm and murmured, “Please Luc, I want you to call the DOD and inquire about my father. I already tried to ask Tony, but he won’t help. I’m counting on you. Please, help me.”

Merde alors. How did he get involved in such a mess? No wonder Tony was so nervous during lunch. He knew Melissa wouldn’t give up easily.

Luc gently patted Melissa’s hand. “We will do our best,” he said, automatically reverting to the no-commitment promise he gave to his patients suffering from incurable disorders.

But what else could he say in desperate cases? He would never lie and make false promises, knowing firsthand the damage lies caused. He vowed that when the time came, he would help Melissa face the truth.

As he raised his head, Luc caught Olivia's questioning gaze and swallowed hard. He'd been able to distract her for a moment. A sweet moment, unfortunately too short. And now?

Had she finally realized her white lie had morphed into quicksand threatening to engulf her? Could he help Melissa discover the truth about her father without hurting her mother—the woman he'd give anything to protect?

****

"I'll drive Melissa home. Don't worry about coming back to get her," Olivia said to Tony as they walked out of the restaurant and waited for the valet to bring her car around. A few feet ahead of them, Luc and Melissa chatted and laughed.

"Be patient with her." Tony put a soothing hand on Olivia's arm. "Last night she asked me to call the DOD for her."

Olivia swiveled toward him. "Oh my God."

"You can't wait till she's twenty-five." Tony sighed and blinked several times. "You may have to tell her sooner."

Olivia's stomach churned, the dormant ulcer resurrected by the new stress. "I've been thinking about it all morning." Actually the thought had pounded her brain like an out of control gong. "But how can I do it, now?"

Tony shook his head. "You have to. The sooner, the better. If you need help I'll be around." He glanced sideways toward Luc and Melissa. "And I have a feeling your French visitor is more than ready to lend a hand too."

"He's been very helpful." Olivia turned her head to where her daughter was standing with Luc.

"And he couldn't take his eyes off you during lunch." Tony chuckled. "Except when he glared at me. If looks could kill…"

"Come on, Tony. Don't exaggerate." Heat crept into Olivia's cheeks.

"I'm certainly not. The man is jealous of me, and that's a fact." Tony shook his wrist. "He almost snapped my arm with his handshaking. Seriously, you should tell him not to worry about our friendship. Unless, he just wants to fool around with you, in which case I'll deal with him."

"Oh Tony, you're so sweet." Olivia took a step forward and opened her arms to hug him.

Tony took a step backward and raised his hands. "Stop there, sweetheart. Your French knight is looking. This time he'd snap my neck, even though it's quite thick. There's a lot of strength under his polished exterior." Tony burst out laughing. "I definitely see how he can make a female heart melt."

"Bug off, Tony. My heart is safe and too cold to melt. Besides, it belongs to Melissa entirely."

"Another mistake, sweetheart. Maybe it's time to change a few things around here."

The valet brought the van around and the four of them settled in. Olivia drove in silence, ruminating over her conversation with Tony. She ground her teeth to avoid screaming at his intolerable advice.

To tell Melissa!

Tell her what? That her father had abused her mother and ordered her to abort. Tell her that her mother had lied to her.

Damn you, Jeremy. After sixteen years, he still inflicted suffering on his victims.

Luc's throaty laughter echoed Melissa's high-pitched giggle from the rear seat and pulled Olivia out of her depressing thoughts. Luc had won her daughter's trust in record time. No surprise there. As usual, his blatant charm worked wonders around female hearts. With an invitation to visit his chateau in France, Melissa would soon adore him.

So far, Luc hadn't extended his invitation to Olivia. Did he still resent her? He'd been so busy all morning extracting more information out of her. By now, he'd probably figured out that Jeremy was Melissa's father. Olivia hadn't missed the somber looks he'd shot her when she'd entered her office and found him there. Tony's presence had complicated matters even more.

When they arrived at the university, Olivia parked her car in her allotted spot at the end of the parking lot. While her passengers got out of the van, she clenched her fingers around the steering wheel, then forced them open and exhaled quietly. She closed her eyes for a couple of seconds.

Considering her jumbled thoughts and churning stomach, they were lucky to have reached CUH without incident. Where was her neatly organized timetable? The to-do list she typed every morning on her computer?

Luc had interfered in every aspect of her life. Somehow he'd touched and affected her daughter, her best friend, and her patients, not to mention her own calm.

She snorted. How could she resent him when she hadn't been able to forget him or replace him? Hadn't he just gone against his own beliefs of the truth-above-all to support her? Or had she misunderstood his meaning?

Now that he knew about Jeremy, wouldn't he understand her reluctance to destroy her daughter's peace of mind? Her fingers tightened on the steering wheel as her recurrent nightmare played behind her closed eyelids. Jeremy meeting Melissa and hurting them both. Or Melissa discovering the truth—and the lies—and resenting her loving mother.

The driver's door opened. Luc extended his hand to help her out. His gaze caressed her face and rested on her mouth. She pressed her lips together to still a quiver.

"Problems again, *chérie?*" His large palm closed over her hand. Heat suffused her arms and throat.

"Unexpected complications." Innumerable ones. She shrugged, willing her body to ignore him, to stop secretly begging for his touch.

"I promised you once that I would help you. I always keep my promises."

"I know." She lowered her lashes, unable to bear the tenderness in his gaze without unveiling her own emotions, feelings she had to sort through and study. "Thank you for distracting Melissa." She craned her neck to watch Tony and her daughter at the other end of the parking lot, already ambling up the stairs leading to the School of Medicine.

"Olivia, you will have to tell Melissa soon."

Tony had said the same thing. She raised her head toward Luc, pleading for his understanding. "I can't. Don't you see? It will destroy us in the process."

His hand cradled her cheek. The tension ebbed with the brush of his fingertips along the line of her jaw.

"Trust me, Olivia. I will be here to help you."

She leaned into the warmth of his palm to savor his touch and extract comfort from his calm strength. He eased her forward and bent over her.

Linking her fingers behind his nape, she molded her lips to his and shut her problems out of her mind. He invaded her mouth, played with her tongue, and stole her breath with his passion. How had she lived for so many years without Luc, without his kisses and his strength?

He rubbed her back, pressing her against him. She felt his arousal and wished they weren't in a parking lot, even a deserted one at this time of the afternoon. She pulled her mouth away to breathe and tucked her head in the hollow of his neck.

"*Mon trésor, ma chérie, tu m'as manqué.* I missed you," he whispered the endearments against her hair.

She missed him too, but didn't dare voice her regret for the time lost. She sighed and bit her inner lip hard, tasting blood. Why was life so complicated? Why couldn't she grab the second chance fate handed her?

Because she still had to protect Melissa, make up for her past mistake until Melissa turned twenty-five.

Kissing Luc wasn't helping.

"Luc, I have a class in an hour. Let's go."

The wind ruffled her hair around her face. Luc reached out and tucked a wayward strand behind her ear. He kissed her again, a deep kiss that dazed her. Her knees weak, she clung to his shoulders and moaned into his mouth. "Please." She didn't know if she was begging him to stop or to make her forget the world with more passion.

"Olivia, I could tell you not to worry, but—"

"But what? Tell me." She didn't like his hesitation.

"Melissa asked me to call the DOD and get her a picture."

"You too?" Olivia stepped back and stared at him. "What are you going to do?"

He shook his head. "I told her I will do my best. I can procrastinate for some time, but I will not lie to her."

"No!" Her breath caught in her chest as she shook her head.

"I told her that dealing with the DOD would take time. But not forever."

"What do you mean? What do you plan to do? You're not going to betray me?"

"Olivia, listen to me—"

"Damn it. Luc, you're still the inflexible, holier-than-thou perfectionist." She couldn't help shouting as she grabbed his arms. "You can't tell her. I'll never forgive you, Luc. Never, if you say a single word. You don't have the right."

"You are correct. I do not have the right to dictate. I am not her relative or yours." Sadness clouded his eyes, quickly replaced by a harshness she'd never seen before. "But you have the right to do it, Olivia. The right and the duty."

The September breeze cooled her skin. Olivia hugged herself. "I will tell her about her father. At the right time."

"The right time?" He shook his head, disapproval in his gaze. "You know Walter Scott was right when he said that when we hide the truth we cannot get out of the mess."

Taken aback, she frowned. "He didn't say that."

"Something about deceit and webs of lies."

Her scowl deepened, and then she pinched her lips and shrugged. "You mean, *Oh what a tangled web we weave, when first we practice to deceive.* Thanks a lot, Luc."

Turning around, she hastened toward the school building. Would there ever be a right time to destroy her daughter's life?

Her eyes blurred, and she tripped as she took the steps two at a time. Luc held her elbow and helped her regain her balance. "Careful."

Would he always be at her side when she needed him? Would she compare to his string of beautiful French mistresses who didn't come with baggage and a complicated past?

Luc kept up with her as she rushed toward her office, her sanity on the brink of collapse. When would this craziness end?

Olivia halted at the sight of Melissa talking to an older man in the hallway. Her daughter turned toward her, a sympathetic smile on her face. “Mom, this is Mr. Rutherford. He’s waiting for Dean McMillan.”

Jeremy’s grandfather.

Chapter Seven

Her feet glued to the floor, Olivia considered the man responsible for Jeremy's reappearance in her life. Tall, rather skinny with white hair and blue eyes, a daunting figure in an elegant suit. He was talking to her daughter.

His great-granddaughter.

For a second the hallway rotated like a kaleidoscope of shadow and light in front of Olivia. She brought her hand to her head, willing her dizziness to fade.

Luc immediately moved next to her and murmured, "Don't worry." He faced the visitor. "May I help you, sir?"

The old man smiled. "As this young lady said, I'm waiting for Dr. McMillan. I am Thomas Rutherford."

"Monsieur Rutherford." Luc extended his hand to the distinguished visitor. "I am Dr. Lucien de Vicour-Michelet, visiting physician at CUH. And this is Dr. Crane, our acting chairman. Dr. McMillan is not here today. Did you have an appointment, sir?

"No. I just stopped to share some more information about my grandson with Dr. McMillan before he leaves on his sabbatical. But Dr. Crane, I have heard about you. Dr. McMillan mentioned you would be handling my grandson's case."

No, no, no. The words lodged in Olivia's throat, strangling her.

She felt Luc's gaze on her. He stepped forward as if to shield her from an invisible blow. "Monsieur Rutherford, after careful consideration of the file you provided, Dr. McMillan and Dr. Crane have asked me to study this case." Self-confidence underlined the polite rebuttal.

Bless you, Luc. He wouldn't allow the old man a chance to discuss their decision.

"Thank you, doctor. I trust you must be an expert in your field." Rutherford nodded his appreciation.

Olivia sent Luc a grateful look, convinced that the Rutherford grandfather sensed the aura of calm authority emanating from her French colleague.

Now what? In spite of her hatred for anything bearing the loathsome name, she couldn't turn her back and walk away. Doc would never forgive her for mistreating an important benefactor of the department.

"This way, Monsieur Rutherford. Dr. McMillan has been kind enough to allow me to use his office in his absence." Luc opened Doc's office and stepped back to let Rutherford enter.

Olivia paused at the door. Seeing her hesitation, Luc waved his hand. "*Après toi*, Olivia. After you."

"I assume Mr. Rutherford would appreciate a private discussion. Melissa and I will be in my office." Olivia didn't want to be here, in Rutherford's presence, and she couldn't bear to see her daughter next to him.

Not now. Not ever.

She grabbed Melissa's hand and backed away from the door.

Luc touched her arm. "I would like you to stay."

She spun toward him. Damn it, why was he forcing her to listen to details she wanted to ignore?

"Please, Olivia," he lowered his voice for her ears only while his guest surveyed the office. "It may be helpful to you." He raised his voice. "Melissa, can you wait in the office of your *maman*, please?"

Melissa nodded. "Bye, Mr. Rutherford. I hope

your grandson feels better."

"Thank you, Melissa."

Luc closed the door behind her and held a chair for Olivia, while he glanced at the grandfather. "Have a seat, sir."

"What a charming daughter you have, Dr. Crane." The old man gazed out of the window, lost in his thoughts. Luc and Olivia respected his silence. "Yes, she's a lovely girl. She reminds me of..." He breathed heavily.

Olivia jerked forward, grasping the arms of her chair with both hands.

"She reminds me of my granddaughter. In fact she's her spitting image." His lips curved down in a bitter line. "Jennie died in a car accident at fifteen. A stupid, reckless accident." His fingers tightened into a fist.

Unable to breathe, Olivia tried to remember. Jeremy had never mentioned a sister.

"Was she driving?" Luc asked with gentle concern.

"No." Rutherford fixed his gaze on Luc, his Adam's apple bobbing up and down. "Her brother was." He lowered his head. Pain furrowed deep lines in his dry skin.

Olivia winced, hit by an unexpected pang of sympathy for the grandfather. "Oh."

"He didn't have his driver's license yet. We hid this fact to protect him. I wouldn't tell you this if you were anyone else but the doctors who are going to treat him," he added, a noticeable warning in his voice.

So Jeremy had always managed to stay out of trouble. Even when he was responsible for his sister's death. His grandfather had protected him, knowing the teenager had been driving without a license. What little compassion Olivia felt a moment ago flew out the window.

Rutherford Senior and Doc expected her to help Jeremy? Why should she do it? Why would Luc burden himself with this case? Let the man pay for the hurt he'd inflicted. Let him rot in a jail. No word of sympathy passed her lips.

"I am sorry for your loss, Monsieur," Luc said, always the noble gentleman.

Rutherford took a deep breath and exhaled. "Seeing your daughter, Dr. Crane, brought back memories. What an amazing resemblance. Now that I think of it, she also looks like my grandson."

That was the last straw. Olivia recovered her calm. She'd had it with the old man's uncomfortable comparisons. "Mr. Rutherford, before we digress any further, can you tell us what brought you here?"

"I wanted to ask Dr. McMillan a favor." Rutherford's piercing eyes came back to her. "My grandson said he refuses to see a shrink. Is there any way you can see him out of here?" He tapped the arm of his chair with his arthritic fingers. "Come to the house. Talk to him there, and—"

"No, sir," Olivia interrupted, her voice firm. "To treat a patient we need to have his written consent. Diagnostic sessions can be done here, at the hospital, or at the Crisis Center. We can't allow exceptions."

The old man's lips tightened. "What if Jeremy doesn't want to come?"

Olivia opened her hands, palms up, and shrugged. "We can't force someone to be treated or assessed against his will." She glanced at Luc, pleased that she'd almost got rid of the Rutherford case. A hint of a smile played on his lips. He understood her so well.

"He must come to see you. He's my only heir. His parents died in Nepal during one of their crazy trips abroad. I'm not going to leave my fortune to Jeremy in his present state of mind. He would waste it in no time." Rutherford snorted in disgust. "Maybe

I should disinherit him."

"I'm sorry, sir." To be honest, she was delighted. If Jeremy refused to come for treatment, her main problem would disappear. One of them anyway. She would still have to convince Melissa to forget about her father's picture.

She stood to signify the end of the meeting.

Apparently not ready to go, Rutherford remained seated in his chair, his back straight, a deep scowl furrowing his forehead.

"I'll have to leave you with Dr. Lucien. I have a class in a few minutes," Olivia said as she gathered her purse and notepad.

Mr. Rutherford snapped his fingers. "That's it. I've found a solution."

"You did?" Olivia dropped back onto her chair, struggling to hide her disappointment. "What's that?"

"I'll threaten to disinherit him and give my money to charity. I worked hard to make my fortune. If only there were someone else left in my family to inherit."

Distress mixed with anger in Olivia's heart. Money. That was all that counted in this family. The only thing Jeremy cared about.

"As you wish, Monsieur," Luc said with a quick glance toward Olivia. She didn't like the visible accusation in Luc's eyes. She was depriving Melissa of her father's family and inheritance. As if Olivia gave a damn about the Rutherfords and their money.

"Yes." The grandfather's lips stretched into a satisfied smile. "Jeremy has never worked. He's used to an easy life. If he has no money to pay his lawyers, he'll realize he can end up in jail. Trust me, he'll come." The old man rose to his feet with a creaking of his knees. "Thank you both for your time."

Luc opened the door for Rutherford. He stepped out just as Melissa sauntered into the hallway. “Mom, at what time are we going home?”

“Lovely girl,” Rutherford mumbled as he stared at her. “You remind me so much of my granddaughter. You don’t look like your mom, though. You probably resemble Mr. Crane.”

“Mr. Crane?” Melissa asked.

“Your father.”

Olivia gasped, hating the man’s sentimentality.

Melissa smiled sadly. “My dad is Joe Madden. He died as a war hero, a long time ago.”

“I’m sorry, Melissa. I’m glad we met today.” He turned around, muttering about an unfair world, and walked down the corridor.

Olivia stabbed his back with a look of revulsion. No matter how old or lonely, the old man was Jeremy’s grandfather.

“Olivia, we need to talk.” Luc touched her shoulder to get her attention. “After your class?”

Right now she needed to dunk her head under cold water to clear her thoughts, but she barely had time to rush to her students. “After the class, I have another patient.”

Luc had helped her maintain her cool during the most difficult situation she’d been confronted with in many years. “We’ll talk later. Thanks for your help.”

For a second, she had the crazy desire to wrap her arms around his neck and ask him to take her away from her problems and her loveless life.

A deep sigh escaped her. Crazy thoughts indeed when she stood in a university hallway with her daughter beside her and students bustling toward their classes.

“Melissa, do me a favor. Stop ambling around in the hallways. You must have some homework to do. Go to my office and stay there until I’m ready to go home.”

"Okay, Mom." Melissa shook her head. "You're really in a lousy mood today. I hope you feel better by the time we go home."

"Melissa," Olivia said in a warning tone.

"Looks like it's going to be a fun night," her daughter mumbled.

"*Au revoir*, Melissa." Luc's smile didn't thaw the frosty atmosphere.

"Hey Luc, why don't you come with Mom to the house? You can talk to her there. You can meet my grandmother. And you'll see the color of the leaves in our countryside. It's so beautiful at this time of the year."

"Olivia?"

Luc waited.

She nodded. "Whatever. See you later." Olivia tossed the word over her shoulder as she strode away. She was used to tackling one problem per day. But today she'd had more than her share.

A problem per hour. How many hours were left before the day would end?

****

An hour later, Luc strolled along the corridor toward Olivia's classroom. She should be out soon. Unable to control his curiosity, he paused in front of the door and peered through the glass pane. Olivia pointed at a screen, the slide showing a diagram and notes. Luc smiled, delighted to see another professional side of her. Olivia, the professor, was poised and calm in spite of the turmoil she'd faced an hour ago.

She turned off the projector and switched the light on, concluding her class. Luc backed against the opposite wall, waiting. A couple of minutes later the door opened, and the students poured out, followed by their professor.

Luc came forward. "Dr. Crane, please, when is your next consultation?" he asked while several students eyed him.

"In a few minutes. I'm on my way, Dr. Luc. Do you want to sit in?"

"Definitely." They hurried away from the crowd of students.

"I don't have time to talk now," Olivia said as they rushed toward the Crisis Center.

"I know." He looked at her with concern, noticing the purple shadows under her eyes. "You must be exhausted physically and mentally."

"I'm used to coping. I'll survive, as long as you respect my decision to protect Melissa and don't interfere."

He didn't want to add to her worries now. "Olivia, I will personally never reveal anything to Melissa. We will discuss it later."

"There will be no more discussion." Olivia stopped before entering the consultation room, propped her fists on her waist, and narrowed her eyes. "Stay out of it. Period."

Luc arched his brow. Without a word, he turned around and opened the door for her.

A young woman waited in a chair, a baby in her arms. She tried to stand when she saw them.

"Please, don't bother, Julia." Olivia gestured to her to remain seated as she settled in a chair across from her. "You brought your baby," Olivia said with a smile.

"I'm sorry. My babysitter was not available today. But it's okay, Brendon's asleep."

"No problem. Julia, I realize you're used to talking with me alone. Dr. Luc is consulting in our hospital. Do you mind if he sits in with us?"

"Not at all, Dr. Crane."

Olivia reached for the medical record on the cocktail table and handed it to Luc who pulled a chair next to her. "This is a follow-up visit for Julia. She's made excellent progress in the last year."

Julia looked adoringly at her baby. "When I think I was about to get rid of him. Now I feel blessed that I had depression when I was pregnant. It forced me to seek help." She cradled the baby tighter and glanced toward Luc. "Dr. Crane has been wonderful to me. She encouraged me to keep my baby and prescribed medication for my anxiety."

Luc smiled his approval.

"How are you feeling now, Julia?" Olivia asked with a gentle tone.

"Great. I started working part-time in a bookstore. I go twice a week and leave my baby with a neighbor. She's very nice."

"Good. What about the migraines?"

"I haven't had one in the last couple of weeks."

"Any panic attacks? Are you still feeling hopeless?"

"No. On the contrary. My boyfriend came back. When he saw his son, he started crying. He said he'd made a huge mistake when he asked me to get rid of the baby. Now he wants us to get married so Brendon can have a real family."

If her arched brow was any indication, Olivia was not convinced. When would she ever accept the fact that a child needed a father as well as a mother?

"What do *you* want, Julia?" Olivia asked in her professional tone.

"I still love him."

"Love is not everything, Julia. You need to be in control of your life and your child's life. Don't surrender your responsibilities to anyone else. Even your baby's father."

Luc scowled, more interested in Olivia's philosophy than in her patient's case—a twisted philosophy in his opinion.

"He's always been good to me, but he panicked and left when I said I was pregnant. I'm going to ask him to prove himself before I say *yes*."

"Very smart decision." Olivia's eyebrow relaxed, and a satisfied smile settled on her lips.

So, *Prove yourself* was the name of the game to win a woman's heart in Olivia's book. Luc crossed his arms on his chest. No problem. Except that he had probably messed up big time on Olivia's scale when he insisted she tell the truth to Melissa.

"Any crying?" Olivia asked her patient.

"Last week, I felt like crying without reason, then I hugged my baby and relaxed."

"Really? Are you still taking your *Zoloft* in the morning?"

"I stopped for a week. I was feeling so good I thought I didn't need it anymore. Then when I started crying for no reason, I took it again."

"Julia, you can't stop your medicine just like that."

"Am I going to take it all my life?"

Olivia shook her head. "When you're ready I will decrease the dose gradually, and eventually we'll stop it. But not yet."

The baby started crying. The young mother raised him against her shoulder and patted his back. "I'm sorry." She pulled a bottle out of her diaper bag and slid the nipple into her son's mouth.

"He's a beautiful baby and big for three months," Olivia said.

"Would you like to hold Brendon, Dr. Crane?" Without waiting, Julia handed baby, bottle, and burp cloth to Olivia.

Olivia cradled the infant against her chest and cooed at him as she brought the bottle to his lips. A smell of milk clung around her, quite endearing. Mesmerized, Luc gazed at her. He had seen her as a loving mother to Melissa, but this image of Olivia with a baby stole his breath.

Pain shot through him as he imagined his little Paul in her arms. She'd have been a fabulous mother...if she'd wanted to give herself a chance. If she could get herself to trust him and stop hiding behind her secrets and self-imposed duties.

Luc swallowed. He'd always known he wanted to make love to her and keep her forever as his wife, but now...

Now he realized how badly he wanted a child.

Their child.

Wake up, mon ami.

He cursed under his breath. Olivia didn't want a husband and certainly not another child. She liked her life as it was.

An empty life. A dull, empty life like the one he'd lived for the last ten years.

Chapter Eight

"I'm done." Olivia stretched her arms up after the door closed behind her last patient. "What a day." As she slumped into her chair, she threw a sidelong glance at Luc. How could he look so dashingly fresh at the end of such a strenuous day? "I wish I could take a shower and climb into bed with a good book."

Actually cuddling with Luc in her lonely bed would top her list of relaxation remedies. She lowered her head to prevent him from noticing any treacherous blush.

Luc sat beside her, his gaze glued to her. "I can drive Melissa home."

She shook her head. "Nope. You don't know my daughter. I'll never hear the end of it if I'm a no-show two days in a row."

"You think so?" Luc dragged his chair closer, peering at her. "Why? Don't you think she loves you and appreciates all that you are doing for her?"

"Of course she loves me, but you know what teenagers are like." Hmm, stupid thing to say. What did he know about teenagers? The only ones he saw were sick kids.

"Olivia, what are you really afraid of?" Luc shifted, and his elbow dug into the chair arm as he angled his head toward her.

"What?" She swiveled to face him. "Luc, don't start." Lord, she'd just daydreamed about him as a lover. Then he'd quashed her fantasy by pulling out his shrink's act.

"I will give you my professional advice for the

last time. Then do what you want." Cupping his chin, he slid his fingers back and forth along his chiseled jaw in a hypnotizing motion.

She'd rather skate her own fingers across his light stubble. "I really don't want your advice." *I want you. God, I want you so much.* How long would she have to keep her emotions tucked in her suit pocket?

But Luc was dead set on giving his opinion. "Olivia, did you have counseling after your bad experience?"

"No, my parents were there for me. They helped and supported me when Melissa was born. I had to adjust to being a mother at eighteen, but in the end everything was great." She smiled and then sighed.

"Everything is obviously not great. You should seek help. Try to be objective." The tender streak in his blue eyes darkened with concern. "Imagine another woman in your position. Don't you think she would need help to assess her problem and find the courage to tackle the situation?"

She frowned at his firm tone. Earlier in the day, she'd gotten defensive when he'd asked a similar question. Not anymore.

During lunchtime, Melissa's comments had hit hard. While Olivia lurked behind a false sense of security, her daughter was making plans that threatened their easygoing life. Besides, in all other areas, Olivia was a doer, used to taking action and control. So why not now, when the most precious person in her life was at stake?

"Maybe you're right." If an acquaintance had told her about a similar problem, she'd advise her to get therapy. "But I can't do it. I mean, not officially. I can't go to any of my colleagues in Cincinnati." Her pulse accelerated at the idea of her story typed on a computer, printed on several sheets of paper, and stored in a file.

Dr. Olivia Crane, the respected professor of Psychiatry seeing a shrink. She might lose her credibility, even her position and her patients, if anyone heard about her personal issues. "I absolutely refuse to have a medical record on this subject." She blew out a small frustrated breath. Her gaze locked with Luc's, willing him to understand.

He interrupted his fingers' annoying motion along his jaws to pinch his chin and study her through narrowed eyes. "Would you allow me to analyze you?" He paused, hesitating for a few seconds. "We would cover only your past history."

She bit her lip, thinking. Could she talk to Luc, let him help her, share his assessment? He was one of the most prominent psychiatrists in the world. And he cared about her and Melissa.

"Can you be objective enough?" she asked as the idea began to sink in.

His eyebrows shot up. "You can stop anytime if I am not objective."

"Sorry. I didn't mean—" She hoped he wasn't insulted.

"I know." He inched away from her and leaned against the back of his chair. "We will not discuss our relationship."

"Luc, you're the best psychiatrist I've ever known."

"*Merci*. I am honored." He acknowledged her compliment with a quick smile and a nod before a serious frown knitted his forehead. "So, what is your decision?"

Maybe it was time for her to stop running away. Time to face the demons of her past. She raised her head to meet his eyes and allowed herself a bitter smile. "Would you like me to sign a written consent?"

He rubbed his knuckles gently against her cheek. "*Non, chérie*. Just trust me for once."

"Go ahead." She held up her hands in surrender.

"We may as well get the initial visit over with, Dr. Vicour-Michelet, although I don't know if my insurance can afford your exorbitant fees."

He gave her a devastating smile. "Consider it a doctor-to-doctor favor." He pushed his chair to face her and linked his fingers together on his lap. "Tell me, what type of childhood did you have?" he asked with the same gentle, professional tone they both used with their patients.

She relaxed against the back of her chair. "A wonderful childhood."

A picture of her parents' house popped up behind her close eyelids. The red brick house where she, and later her daughter, grew up. She raked her fingers through her hair, rested her cheeks in her cupped hands and smiled. Her parents had given her a great deal of emotional stability.

"My father was much older than my mother. He lost his first wife and two children in a car accident. It took him years to recover. At fifty, he married an Italian nurse twenty years younger than him. He was delighted by my birth. I was loved and spoiled."

"You went to college at UC?"

Olivia glanced at Luc. His legs crossed, he sat straight in his chair, the all-professional shrink, asking questions, seeking answers he already knew just to analyze her expressions when she talked.

"Nope. They were suffocating me with love and attention. I wanted my freedom." She groaned and pursed her lips, appalled by the ungratefulness of her youth. Her parents had protected her, but all she'd done was run away. "Lord, I hope Melissa doesn't feel the same."

His expression controlled, Luc fixed her with a penetrating gaze. "We will save the comments for later. Concentrate on your story. What did you do next?"

She twisted her fingers in her lap. "I joined

Northwestern premed." She'd never told Luc she'd lived in Chicago. One more thing that belonged to the nightmarish past. "Dad was very proud. Mom cried when I left. The day after I arrived at Northwestern, I met—" She paused unable to pronounce the loathsome name and squinted, seeking comfort. Luc reached over and squeezed her hand.

"You met Jeremy Rutherford. What was he like?"

She exhaled and closed her eyes. The picture in the folder flitted in her mind. "Handsome, funny, attractive. I was young and naive, like all the girls competing to be noticed by the dashing senior." She blinked, overwhelmed by her own folly. "After a month, he came to talk to me in the cafeteria and invited me to a party in his apartment." She threw a glance at Luc. Would he still respect after hearing the sordid details?

"How did you feel about it?" His eyes narrowed, Luc uncrossed his legs and leaned forward.

"I was thrilled." She shook her head. "Can you believe I was so stupid?"

"What happened at the party?" he asked.

"Everyone was drinking. Not beer. Heavy stuff. I was eighteen, underage, but I was so proud to be treated like a grownup. Somehow I ended up in bed with him. My first time." She chewed on her lips and suppressed a gag as Jeremy's alcohol-tinged breath invaded her memory. How could she have found it exhilarating at the time? She scrunched her nose in disgust.

"How did you feel about it?" Luc's strangled breathing reached her, almost as loud as his words.

She knew the basic question of psychiatric diagnosis. *How did you feel about it*? Luc would ask it over and over again. But she wondered if hearing the answer would hurt him. She spared him a glance.

Nothing betrayed his feelings. Not a blink of the eyes, not a deeper crease in his frown. But he was flicking his pen between his fingers.

"I fell in love with him right away and moved in with him a week later. How naïve could a girl be?" Her hand flew to her mouth to stifle a gasp as she thought about Melissa. Would her daughter follow in her footsteps?

"Leave Melissa out of it. Concentrate on yourself."

Luc must have guessed her thoughts. He had an uncanny knack for reading his patients.

"How did you feel when you moved in with him?"

"At first I was so proud to be with this popular guy. But I had a hard time studying at his place. Too noisy with the music and the partying. And I hated lying to my parents who thought I was still living in the dorm. My first semester grades were a disaster, but I couldn't stay away from him."

She slouched into her chair with a sigh. Guilt needled her. Guilt about her parents, her daughter, and Luc, who listened stoically to details that probably offended him. She'd moved in with a jerk in the blink of an eye but later rejected the man who loved her.

"When did things deteriorate?" Luc asked with a calm, almost soft tone of voice.

"Luc, I can't continue." She glanced at him. His eyes fixed on her, he studied her impassively. "There are things I can't tell you. Especially you." Covering her face with her hands, she rubbed her forehead, hoping to ease the tension that drummed against her temples.

"I am a psychiatrist, Olivia. I have heard it all." His fingers unclasped her hands from her face and gently moved them to her lap.

"But I will lose your respect. I can't afford that."

She clasped her fingers. Her nervousness escalated. Anxiety, shame, guilt played a scary dance in her heart. Was this how her patients felt when pouring out their souls in her office?

"Never, *chérie*. We have all made mistakes in our lives." Cupping her chin, he tilted her head toward him. "I am not here to judge. Just to help you assess your feelings."

She wanted to hug him and thank him for his kindness. He dropped his hands and resumed his professional attitude. She sighed. Since she'd started, she might as well finish.

"After three months, he said I didn't excite him anymore, but his friend was interested. I said no. He was rude and said I was a stupid kid. I cried, then threw up and was sick. He left me in peace. But after that, things changed. He'd sleep with me, then bully me. In a way, I was addicted to him. I stayed, hoping he'd change and love me again."

She scanned Luc's face, searching for a sign of disparagement. His features remained blank, but a tic played in his jaw. He leaned toward her and patted her hand.

"When did you find out you were pregnant?"

"A month later. I thought Jeremy would be happy to have a baby, and we'd get married right away." She stifled a grunt of disgust. *Stupid, naïve girl.*

"But he wasn't."

"He slapped me and told me I did it on purpose to trap him. Then he said he would forgive me if I got rid of it." The words lumped in her throat as she recalled the fury in Jeremy's eyes. Get rid of her baby. Her beautiful Melissa. She stroked her cheek, still feeling the sting of his slap. A wave of humiliation burned her face. "He gave me money and the address of a doctor who had helped his girlfriends before."

"Did you go?"

"I couldn't. At home I was brought up with respect for life." She lowered her eyelids with a murmur of thanks to her parents. Without their moral code, she might have given in and lost her child. "When he found out I didn't go to his doctor—" She choked unable to continue.

"What did he do?" Luc touched her shoulder. "Olivia, can you continue, or would you like to stop now?"

Olivia tried to control her erratic breathing. "He slapped me again and again." She squeezed her eyes shut. It was awful telling Luc these things she'd kept hidden for so long. "I had to protect my baby. I doubled over when he raised a fist."

The terrible memories flooded her mind. "He punched my head, knocked me down and kept hitting my back." She hugged herself and rocked as the words tumbled from her mouth.

"When I remained crouched on the floor, wrapped over myself like a ball, he pulled me by my hair, dragged me to the door, and opened it. Then he took the money from my purse and threw it in my face, yelling for me to go to hell. He shoved me out, and I started walking in the snow." She laced her fingers in her lap to keep them from shaking as she fastened her gaze on Luc.

"What do you mean *in the snow*?"

His blue eyes flared with a dangerous glint. The pen clutched in his hands snapped into two pieces. She cringed at his expression. If Jeremy were here at this moment, Luc would have knocked him down.

"There was a snowstorm that night. I kept walking, trying to reach the school. I fell." Her throat constricted, the terrible night playing in her mind like a horror movie. "I thought about my parents. Asked for their forgiveness and prayed for a miracle." She swallowed, and tears wet her cheeks.

Luc leaned toward her. With the tips of his finger, he wiped the moisture. “I’m sorry, *chérie.* I’m so sorry.”

In spite of her emotion, she almost smiled. Luc had lost his objectivity. She grabbed his hand, willing him to forget the past and kiss her. Now. She needed his lips and his strength like a healing balm to soothe her pain. Very gently, he pushed her back into her chair.

She tilted her head and lowered her eyelashes, her clasped hands squeezed between her trembling knees. “A car stopped, and a man and his wife came over to help me up. They took me to their house and told me to call my mom. That man was Tony.”

Luc frowned. “Dr. Burke?”

“Yes. I owe him big time. My parents became good friends with him. When he lost his wife to cancer a few years ago, I encouraged him to apply to CUH.”

“I see.” Luc scowled and fixed his pad. “I thought...”

“I know. He’s a good man. He’s had his share of suffering.”

Luc’s gaze rested on her and he nodded. “I guess you help each other. A sort of big brother?”

She almost smiled at the relief underlying his question. “My best friend.” She wouldn’t elaborate, but the digression helped her collect herself. She inhaled, glad to be done with the harsh recollection.

Luc raked his hair, messing the dark strands, and then smoothed them with the palm of his hand. “Back to your story.”

“My parents brought me home and helped me. They raised Melissa while I went to UC and got my degrees. I never went back to Chicago.”

“And Melissa still lives with your parents. Yes?”

“With my mother. My father died two years ago. I thought about bringing her with me when I got an attending position, but I worked long hours and night shifts. It didn't seem fair to leave her with babysitters. I visit several times a week. It's only an hour's drive."

"So that's where you disappeared on weekends when we were together. You can't believe how jealous I was when you said you had other commitments."

She arched her eyebrow. "Having trouble remaining detached from the case, Dr. Luc?" The psychiatrist in her couldn't help the sarcastic comment. "Now, you know firsthand why we can't treat relatives or friends."

"*Touché*." He chuckled and blew her a kiss. "I promise to do better from now on, Dr. Crane. You are too good a psychiatrist for me to indulge in such a mistake."

She sighed and relaxed.

Luc jotted more notes on his notepad. "How old was Melissa when she first asked about her dad?"

"Five."

"Why didn't you gently explain that her mommy had left her daddy because he had problems?"

"When she asked me if her daddy had died at war like her friend's dad, I thought the story of a war-hero father was a protection against her real father."

Until recently. Olivia bit her lip as she remembered her rude awakening at today's lunch. Melissa longing for a picture of her father so badly. Oh God.

"Olivia, he didn't even know he had a child. He probably forgot about you. Why were you so scared when Melissa was a little girl?"

"I heard from him. Just before you left for France." She swallowed hard, fear still clear in her memory.

"You did?" He cradled her hand, to protect her

against the invisible but omnipotent bastard.

"He met the only friend I still had in Chicago and started talking about the past. He suddenly turned sentimental, asked about me and wanted an address. She told him she lost track of me years ago. But it scared me enough to keep hiding Melissa."

"And enough to tell me you didn't want to see me anymore, right?" He arched an ominous eyebrow.

"Hey, you're not objective now."

"Sorry. I keep forgetting my patient is an expert psychiatrist." He smiled. "How do you feel about Jeremy now?"

"What a question! I hate him. I want him to pay for the hurt he'd caused me and many other women apparently."

"Are you still afraid of him?"

"I love my daughter. He can hurt me through Melissa." Her foot tapped at the carpet in a jerky motion.

"Olivia, he can't take her away from you. She is too old for that, and you are a successful psychiatrist, not a naïve young girl. You can't be afraid of Jeremy now."

It was true. She was a dedicated doctor, a prominent university professor with a well-established career. And yet her heart still pounded at the mention of Jeremy's name.

"Olivia, what are you really afraid of?"

"Stop repeating that question. You're getting on my nerves."

"You have not answered yet. Are you afraid of hurting Melissa?"

"Yes. When I tell her the truth, in a way I'll be killing the father she adores. Can you imagine her disappointment? How can I tell her he didn't want her? She may even think I kept my baby and took care of her out of duty, not love. Oh Luc, she'll feel rejected, unwanted."

"I know it may hurt her, but we will help her."

"We?" Frustration raged inside her. She bit her lip not to tell him he didn't know the *ABC*s of parenthood.

"Yes, I won't let you do it alone." His eyes shone with sincerity.

He'd lost a son and treated others' children, but he'd never raised a child, coped with the daily problems.

Would a real father hurt his daughter in the name of the truth? She snorted. The real father had tried to get rid of his daughter. Even without personal experience, Luc was by far a better example of fatherhood than any man she knew.

"We may create new problems. Do you think she'll be able to stand the sight of a man after that? Remember some of your cases. Don't you think the truth will make her doubt the sincerity of any young man she meets?"

"With good therapy, she can get over it. I am confident we can help her. How about you, Olivia? Are you afraid of losing Melissa's love?"

Tears pooled in her eyes and clogged her throat. "She's all I have, Luc." He reached over and smoothed her hair. "I can't afford to lose her. She won't forgive me. How can I take that risk?"

"You are a strong woman."

"You can't understand. I..." She stood and turned away from him, unable to continue her sentence. She'd given up on personal relationships years ago to surround Melissa with love, an exclusive affection so strong her daughter wouldn't miss a father's presence.

"*Chérie*, don't be too hard on yourself."

She threw a glance of regret at Luc. He straightened and gathered her in his arms. She dropped her forehead on his shoulder, and he pressed her against his hard body. With gentle strokes on her back, he eased the stiffness in her muscles but didn't try to kiss her.

An uncontrollable longing built in her heart. She shuddered, wanting to be loved, held and protected. Yes, protected even from herself. Happiness was an impossible dream as long Melissa was still too young to accept the past without suffering.

Olivia had sacrificed so much to make up for the mistakes of her youth. For how long would she have to forgo her own happiness for her duty toward Melissa?

Chapter Nine

Olivia loved her mother to death, but at the moment she wanted to scream her frustration at her beaming Mama. It was obvious Marianna Crane had fallen in love with Luc the moment she'd seen him, or more precisely at the very minute he bent over and kissed the back of her hand with an "*Enchanté, madame*."

"I'm delighted to meet you, Luc. Please have a seat. Where have I put my glasses? Melissa, bring the tray of hors d'oeuvres from the kitchen. Olivia, can you serve the drinks? Luc, what can I get you?"

Mama bustled with energy, the way she always did before starting a new project. Seeing her fussing around Luc, Olivia was afraid to guess the name of the new project—her mother's ongoing goal.

But Olivia was too tired to protest or interfere. Two hours ago, when she'd voiced her panic at the possibility of losing Melissa's love, Luc had cut short their session. He'd told her she needed to relax now that she'd exteriorized her real fear. They'd continue next week. Olivia had been so exhausted, she'd let Luc drive them in her van.

"May I help with the drinks?" Luc offered.

"Of course. Make yourself at home," Mama purred.

Dropping onto one of the overstuffed chairs of the old-fashioned living room, Olivia rested a moment. She liked coming home to her mother's. The warm aroma of potpourri soothed her rattled nerves. Tonight, the garlic and nutmeg smell of Mama's masterpiece roast emanated from the kitchen. Her mother had sharpened her tools to conquer their guest.

Olivia recognized the symptoms. Good dinner, good drinks, good stories. Luc wasn't going to leave unscathed tonight, not when her mother wanted Luc's heart for her daughter.

Mama turned toward her. Eyes narrowed, she signaled to Olivia to follow her into the office. "I need you for a second," Marianna ordered with a you-failed-big-time look.

Olivia braced herself for the worst.

As soon as they stepped into the office, Mama closed the glass double doors behind her, spun around to face Olivia and pointed to the door. "This Luc, is he the French boy you dated when you were in med school?"

Mama's scowl promised her lecture was going to be worse than Olivia had expected.

"The one you never wanted to bring home to meet your mama and dad?" Marianna propped her fists on her hips.

Olivia took a deep breath and exhaled. "Yes." It would be a long discussion, all right.

"And you sent him packing? And you let us believe he was no good? Olivia, are you crazy or what?" Marianna snatched a chocolate from a crystal bowl and popped it into her mouth.

"Mom!" Olivia scowled and took a step toward the door.

"Oh no. I have to tell you what I think. *Madonna mia*, you are a great doctor, but as a smart woman...*phht*." Her mother cut the air with her hand. "Any uneducated Italian girl would know that when she meets such a handsome, nice, good-mannered..." Her mother paused for a second to catch her breath and launched again. "Intelligent, famous, wealthy..." She stopped, at a loss for adjectives, and glanced toward the living room for more inspiration.

"Mom, I get your point."

"I'm not finished. He came back. Now you have a second chance. Don't lose it, girl. For once, listen to your mother and keep him. You understand, Olivia?" Mama threw another chocolate into her mouth, chewed on it and then clucked her tongue.

"I understand, Mama. But you have it wrong. I don't think Luc wants to get married, and I'm not ready. I need to see Melissa settled first."

Her mother flung her hands in the air. "*Santa Maria*, help me. Not ready? At thirty-five? You want to wait until you're fifty? And sixty pounds overweight like me? Since when does the daughter marry before her mother?"

"I didn't say Melissa should marry. Just be out of college with a good degree and settled in her career." She smiled gently at her mother, trying to pacify her. "Besides, you know my case is special."

"Special. Why?" Mama shook her head and slapped her thigh. "Olivia Maria Crane, do you think you're the only girl who went through a lousy experience? It happens to many girls, but they move on. My father beat my mother every time he drank. During those days in Napoli, a woman couldn't survive without a husband. My mama stayed with him, but I left home, came to America and met your dad. He certainly didn't want to get married after the sad accident. I was pretty at the time. I made him change his mind." Mama reached for another chocolate.

Olivia chuckled. "You're still pretty, Mama. If you could only stop gorging on chocolate, you'll be healthy too. I'm afraid about Melissa learning—"

"So what if she learns her father's a rotten ass? She'll hate him. Big deal. She'll love you more for protecting her." Her mother stood on tiptoe to pat her cheek. "*Bambina*, it's a great time you think about yourself for a change. Grab him without hesitation." She tugged at Olivia's hand and walked toward the door. "I'll be watching you tonight. I'll keep Melissa out of the way, and I want to see some action."

"You're kidding." Olivia sighed. Now she knew why she'd never brought Luc to meet her parents. Mama would have bought the ring herself, handed it to Luc and watched while he slid it on her daughter's finger.

They joined Luc and Melissa in the living room. Mama crossed her hands on her ample chest. "Luc, Olivia told me so much about you. I feel like I've known you forever."

"*Merci.*" Luc nodded, a smile curving his lips. "*Madame* Marianna, now that I have met you, I understand why your daughter and granddaughter are so lovely."

Mama giggled. "Please call me Marianna. We're not formal here." Tugging at Melissa's hand, she ushered her toward the kitchen and winked at Olivia before walking out.

Hands on her hips, Olivia scowled at Luc. "You know, you are a darn flatterer."

Luc burst out laughing. "*Non, ma chère,* I am a gallant Frenchman who appreciates beauty. Did your mother give you a lecture?"

"Something like that. Why, did you hear her?"

"No." His blue eyes glittered with amusement. "But I noticed her determined look when she ordered you into the office and your flustered expression when you came back."

Disgusting. She'd yet to see him stop acting like an expert shrink and just once, let a look or a move go by without analyzing it.

"My mother showers me with life lessons as she calls them." A glance toward the kitchen reassured her that Marianna was too busy with the meal preparation. Nonetheless, Olivia lowered her voice. “I’m used to her speeches and don’t pay attention anymore,” she said with a shrug.

“Too bad. And here I thought you would obey her and be nice to me tonight.” His lips curled into his trademark smile.

“Luc!”

“What? I have the blessing of your *maman* to court you. I plan to take full advantage.”

She laughed and felt carefree, her problems set aside for the moment. “You’re incorrigible.” Her session with Luc had definitely helped her relax. She still had to talk to her daughter. After hearing Tony’s, Luc’s and Mama’s admonitions, the need to inform Melissa niggled at her mind, but she was determined to enjoy a fun evening.

“Can I fix you a drink? Manhattan still your favorite?” Luc walked to the glass credenza where an ice bucket and bottles were neatly aligned.

“You remember?”

He arched an eyebrow. “I would never forget anything about you. Not the drinks or food you like. Not the way you walk or smile or kiss.” He handed her a glass and captured her eyes. Raw desire smoldered in his gaze. “Or how you cuddled in my arms after we made love.” He murmured the last sentence, sending a wave of heat up to her throat and face. He raised his glass and clicked it against hers. “*A la tienne.* To you. May all your wishes come true.”

Her wishes? Her very secret wishes?

Oh God, I hope he never guesses what they are. She regarded him above the rim of her glass and blushed. Charming blue eyes, a devilish smile, chiseled angles in a most handsome masculine face, and a muscled body that promised delightful caresses. Was he the illusion of her desperate mind or a fabulous second chance knocking on her door?

"Cheers," she whispered as fire burned in her belly.

I want my second chance. So badly.

Luc sat beside her on the blue velvet sofa. He extended his arm behind her and sucked in a breath of relief when she didn't scoot away. Her perfume engulfed him with a delicate fragrance of jasmine and orange blossoms. Olivia was finally learning to relax in his presence. A huge step forward. "I am glad you were expecting an old boring visiting physician."

"What? Why?" She looked at him as if she doubted his sanity.

"Because if you had known it was me, you would have withdrawn the invitation, and I would have continued to waste my life away from you."

Her mouth rounded in an *O*. He inched forward, his eyes trailing the contour of her luscious lips. *Easy Lucien. She's a skittish one.* With supreme effort, he wrenched his gaze away.

"Luc, I can't think about a relationship until Melissa—"

"I know." He took a small frustrated breath and cleared his throat to force the words out. "And I am not ready for commitment either." How could he allow himself to lie when he detested lies, when all he hoped for was to keep her with him forever? But he wouldn't let her trample on his feelings as she did a long time ago. "How about sharing some fun? The way we did ten years ago before I turned sentimental and stupid."

"Some fun?" She frowned and looked at him, shock written all over her face. "You mean...a fling?"

"Fling? I don't know this word, but I like it."

"You've got to be kidding." She hissed through pursed lips and scooted away from him, her abrupt movement molding the silk blouse over her generous breasts.

Luc chugged down his drink, his patience a fragile thread about to snap. He shot a glance toward the corridor leading to the kitchen. Taking the glass from her shaking hand, he set both drinks on the cocktail table. Melissa's and her *grandmère's* chatter reassured him. He trusted Marianna to stay away for as long as she could.

"I will show you what I mean, *chérie*."

He bent toward Olivia, cradled her nape with his hand and brought her face close to his. Before she could utter a sound, he slanted his mouth over hers and enfolded her soft lips, slowly brushing and fondling, while his fingers raked her hair. He'd kissed her twice since he came back, and each time he'd kept a tight rein on his passion. No more. He wanted to show her what they both had missed for so long.

With the tip of his tongue he pressed against her teeth. She sighed. He took advantage to play and taste the trace of Manhattan in her sweet mouth. Her moan fueled his ardor. *Love me, chérie. Love me as I love you.*

He sucked her tongue into his own mouth and led a savage dance around it. As she leaned into him, her nipples peaked against his chest. He flexed his fingers impatiently, opened his palm around her soft mound...and heard Marianna's voice.

"Dinner's ready."

He fisted his hand and straightened up at the same time Olivia lurched away from him and rubbed her lips. She looked at him with dazed eyes. He reached for her half full glass and handed it to her.

For how long would he have to cope with more restraint and contrived interruptions until he got her to realize she needed him? Maybe loved him? But every time he thought of her with *forever* in mind, his hopes were dashed. He shook his head. As long as Olivia worried about telling the truth to her daughter, no future was possible with her.

To think he'd helped so many patients during his career. Why couldn't he help himself and the woman he loved? He downed the rest of his drink, then refilled and swallowed it in a single gulp.

"Luc, Olivia, over here. We are waiting in the dining room."

He offered his hand to Olivia. She emptied her glass, and he helped her up, keeping his arm around her waist to make sure she was steady on her feet. "*Ça va?*"

"No, I'm not fine." She kicked off her shoes, wriggled her toes and exhaled slowly. "There'll be no more of your brand of fun. Understood?"

"Believe me I know how you feel right now." *Frustrated and hungry for more.* His blood still roared in his ears.

She eased out of his hold, raised her head and walked to the dining room. A delicious smell of roasted meat wafted toward them.

"Before we eat I'd like to say grace." Marianna crossed her hands and recited, "Lord, bless our food and those who are about to eat it." She pointedly looked at Olivia. "And Lord, please give wisdom and happiness to those who so badly need them."

Luc stifled a smile as he kept his gaze fixed on Olivia's pinched mouth. He hadn't set foot in a church in ages, but he heartily responded *amen* while she glared at him.

Olivia's mother believed in good cooking. She served everyone generous portions. After he savored a few bites, Luc lavished his hostess with compliments that won him an ecstatic grin from a beaming Marianna and a scowl from Olivia.

Why couldn't she believe that he sincerely appreciated the scrumptious meal and her mother's hospitality?

Melissa asked endless questions about France.

Luc gladly regaled her with descriptions of Paris and the French countryside.

"Thank you, Luc. I can't wait to visit Paris and the many chateaux," Melissa said with a beaming smile.

Olivia's lovely features finally relaxed into a peaceful smile at her daughter's interest.

An hour later, satiated and pleased with his evening, Luc agreed he'd visit often. "Marianna, you are the best cook I have ever met," he said as he licked the last traces of chocolate pudding from his spoon.

"Thank you, Luc." She patted his hand and glanced at Olivia. "I'm writing a cookbook with all my recipes. In case you can't come all the way here, Olivia may cook something easy for you."

"Sure, Mom. As if I have the time. We should leave now, Luc. I'm exhausted. Sorry Mom, I won't be able to help with the clean up."

Olivia hugged her mother and daughter. Luc kissed them on the cheeks three times.

At the door, Melissa pulled on Luc's sleeve. "Can I ask you a favor?"

"Of course." He looked at her, hoping she wouldn't mention her fictitious dad again.

"We have the father-daughter dance at school in three weeks. Would you be my father for the night?"

His heart melted for the sweet teenager. "I would be honored, Melissa." He opened his arms and hugged her.

And he cursed her natural father.

How could he ask Olivia to break her daughter's heart by revealing the identity of an unworthy father?

For a moment he questioned the logic of pushing her to reveal the truth, an ugly revelation that would cause so much hurt to everyone involved.

Including himself.

Chapter Ten

Olivia pressed her head against the headrest of her car seat and closed her eyes. She couldn't deny she'd had a lovely evening in spite of her mother's lecture. One more or less wouldn't bother Olivia. She'd stopped paying attention to her mama's words of wisdom, although tonight she'd been more impatient, with Luc in the next room.

Talk about Luc and his stupid idea of fun. His scorching kiss had shaken her to the core. She'd forgotten she was in her mother's living room and even forgotten her problem with Melissa. To think she'd been ready to slip down on the sofa and let him fondle her as if they were a pair of college kids. Her body still tingled. All because of a kiss.

But what a kiss.

Olivia wrapped her arms around herself. What if he tried to spend the night with her? Would she let him?

"Are you cold?" Luc asked.

"Huh?"

"I can turn up the heat?"

"No, it's fine." As usual Luc was too attuned to her moods and reactions.

"I had a great time at your mother's. She is such a nice lady." He rubbed his stomach and chuckled. "And a good cook."

"I know I have to watch my diet around her."

He chuckled. "You are beautiful, Olivia. You don't have to worry about dieting."

She smiled, pleased with the compliment. Last night she'd taken a good look at her face and wondered if ten years had aged her much in Luc's eyes. Not that it made a difference, of course.

Be honest, you want him to admire you. To find you desirable.

Luc kept the conversation light during the long trip. He stopped in front of her apartment building, walked her to the door, but refused to come in when she invited him up for a last drink.

"Too late now. Besides, if I come...hmm. Let's not tempt the devil as they say in my country. You need your sleep." He blew her a kiss and turned to leave. "I will keep your van and pick you up tomorrow."

Luc hadn't even tried to stay with her. A bit miffed, she huffed and promised herself to stop thinking of him and devote more time to her work.

An hour later, still awake, Olivia tossed in her bed, Luc's striking face smiling at her.

You did it again, Dr. Crane. She'd deleted a ten-year code of good behavior and stern resolutions when he walked into her office and kissed her three times.

Lord, she knew she couldn't resist his sex appeal. She'd melted in his arms the moment he touched her. But it wasn't just his good looks and kisses she craved now. She'd learned to appreciate his strength, his kindness and his continuous attentions.

Why had he come back? Why?

Forgotten sensations prickled her skin. She remembered what it was like to have Luc snuggled against her, to lay her head on his naked chest and hear his heartbeat, to drift off nestled in his arms.

Admit it. You love him.

What was she going to do now? How could she live and work with him every day and feign indifference?

Get him back. He loved you ten years ago.

But what about Melissa? She couldn't forget Melissa. Maybe she could get Luc to love her again, and understand her reasons for keeping the truth from Melissa, and...

Darn, she punched her pillow and went to fetch a sleeping pill and a glass of water. Her phone rang. Annoyed, she wondered if there was an emergency at the Crisis Center. "Hello. Dr. Crane speaking."

"*Chérie*, I have a big problem." His laughing voice contradicted the statement.

"What's wrong?"

"I can't sleep. Can you diagnose my ailment?"

"Bug off, Luc. You scared me."

"Okay, I will tell you what is wrong with me, and you will give me the treatment."

"Treatment for what?"

"For my insomnia, Dr. Crane. Here are my symptoms. I am thinking about you, tossing in bed and wishing I had stayed with you."

"Oh." The single syllable lodged in her throat. She'd experienced the same symptoms. And the only treatment would be...

"The only cure is to take you in my arms. I can come back if you ask me to," he purred in her ear.

She bit her lip hard to avoid saying yes. *Yes, come.* They were both experienced physicians, and she agreed it would be an excellent cure. He would come all the way to her apartment because he wanted her now. As much as she wanted him. She would settle for a fling. And in six months he would leave, and she would cry for months as she did long time ago.

Never. She'd never settle for a fling. He could shove his idea of fun down his throat. She looked at the pill in her hand and sighed. "Ever heard of *Zolpidem*, Dr. Lucien? Take one with a big glass of water. Good night."

She smiled at his sharp intake of breath and

slowly put the receiver in its cradle. From now on, she'd have her own agenda. Seduce and conquer.

My dear Luc, I want you, but on my own terms.

****

The week went by at meteor speed as far as Olivia was concerned. With Doc leaving on Sunday for his sabbatical, she spent many hours locked in his office discussing administrative issues. She hadn't seen much of Luc. He had now taken over Doc's consultations. In addition, he'd started teaching an advanced class on mental disorders.

On Friday afternoon Luc had called to remind her of her appointment with him for her second session. He'd insisted they use one of the consultation rooms to talk in a neutral atmosphere without interruption.

When she strode to the Crisis Center and entered the room, Luc was already there. Sitting behind the desk, he sifted through papers. He closed the folder and stood to greet her.

"Have a seat. How was your day?" he asked in his impersonal physician's voice as he sat in the chair next to hers. She smiled, amused by the touch of formality.

"Good day. No special emergency. What's that?" She pointed to the folder he'd dropped on the table.

"Your file."

"My—?" Her tongue froze on the word. "You put what I told you in writing?" Panic surged to her throat, and she wrestled to control it.

"Not what you told me." He tilted his head in an I-know-better-than-that, and she felt sorry for doubting his discretion. "Only my perceptions of your feelings. It's just a few pages for you to read and shred right away if you like. Not medical records."

She nodded, grateful that he went to the trouble of typing the report himself. "Thanks."

"Tell me, how did you feel after we talked last week?"

"Relieved. Better than I've felt in a long time. Don't say 'I told you so' but you were right." He didn't say it, but she glimpsed a smirk before he suppressed it. "Now I suppose you want me to talk about what happened after I left Chicago." She knew the sequence of a routine consultation.

He nodded. "Exactly. When your parents picked you up from Tony's place."

"Only Mom came. I asked her not to tell my father. For three months I couldn't get myself to say anything to him."

"Why?"

"Because I was afraid to disappoint him."

"Did you think that he would stop loving you because you made a mistake?"

"Uh, no, but...yes." She looked into Luc's eyes and saw the parallel he was establishing. She was still afraid to lose someone's love now because of a past mistake. "I see what you're getting at."

Luc shook his head and smiled. "You are a patient, right now. Leave the diagnosis to me." Serious again, he nodded for her to continue.

"Dad noticed that I was depressed. He thought it was due to flunking my exams." She bit her lip and lowered her head. *Dear Dad*. She'd always been the apple of his eye. "He tried to reassure me that the next year would be better at UC." Thinking about her father and his kindness brought a surge of tickling to her eyes. She blinked several times to suppress her tears.

"When I started crying, he knew there was something else and gently probed. I spilled the whole thing in one breath."

Luc hadn't stopped studying her features while she poured out her soul. He probably reached his conclusion as he jotted some notes on his pad. "And your dad understood, right?"

She chuckled, a laugh that sounded bitter to her ears. "First, he said he was going to kill the son of a bitch. Then he wanted to sue him. Then he took me in his arms and said he couldn't wait to be a grandfather. He and Mom tried their best to make me forget my Chicago experience. They lavished me with tenderness. Later, they took excellent care of Melissa."

"Did they worry about the opinion of their friends and neighbors?"

"Not really. Mom cut the gossip by saying it was an unfortunate but lovely mistake. And nobody dared to question her. My dad was the town's respected pediatrician." Olivia shrugged and dismissed the idea with a flip of her hand. "I went to school at UC. For four years, I drove back and forth. When I was accepted into medical school, we realized I wouldn't have the time to drive. Dad rented an apartment for me."

Luc didn't comment. He'd seen her little studio. A very impersonal place with no pictures or signs of a daughter.

"You didn't try to take Melissa with you?"

"It wouldn't have been fair to transplant her from the comfortable big house in the countryside to a tiny apartment in downtown Cincinnati. Her loving grandmother was always home for her while I'd have had to leave her with babysitters. The arrangement was hard on me but so much better for her. And the school system was by far more superior in our small town than in downtown Cincinnati."

"Why did you choose to keep your daughter a secret from your friends?"

She fidgeted, annoyed by the question. "I told you, I was afraid. Someone may have known a friend of a friend of Jeremy's. I just couldn't take any chances at him finding out about Melissa's existence."

"And when we dated?" He arched his brows, his gaze fixed on her.

"Stop here, Luc. You're getting personal. I won't discuss my relationships. Any of them." She crossed her arms, in full control of her emotions now.

"Them?" His eyes narrowed under his scowl.

"Luc!"

"Okay." His hand raised, he pacified her with a conciliating gesture. "But you did tell McMillan at one point in time, yes?"

"When I accepted the position at CUH, I mentioned I had a daughter. I didn't volunteer any information. No one asked details about my private life. Tony knew of course."

"And now? Would you worry about people, I mean, friends or colleagues meeting Melissa?"

She thought about the question carefully. "Now?" She bit her lip, thinking about Melissa's loveliness and maturity. "No, I really don't mind."

"But you worried when I found out?"

She shrugged. "Only because it triggered too many questions on your part. Otherwise, I'm proud to introduce her to my acquaintances."

"Good." Luc relaxed against the back of his chair and smiled. "I agree with you. I would be very proud of her if she were mine." He leaned forward. "What if someone, a friend of Jeremy's or a relative of his, recognizes her?"

She fixed a questioning look on him. "The grandfather?"

"Yes."

"I don't want him to...to make contact with her. I can't even stand the idea."

"Why, Olivia? The old man would not hurt her."

Luc was right. Rutherford Senior would cherish his only great-granddaughter. "He seemed to like her a lot. He'd probably love her if he knew her identity." Olivia rubbed her throat, a new guilt spiking her heart.

"If the grandfather offers his protection and affection to Melissa would you accept it?"

Would she accept the old man's affection for her daughter? Olivia laced her hands together and swallowed. Would she let him grant them his protection against Jeremy?

She closed her eyes, thinking hard about this new facet of the situation.

Yes, she should.

She opened her eyes and stared at Luc. He was a damn good psychiatrist. "I think I'm going to talk to Melissa."

"Are you sure you are up to it?"

"I can't afford to wait too long. I need one more session with you to plan what I will say. I want her relaxed and in a good mood when I talk to her. This weekend I'll take her shopping for her party. I'll spoil her. New dress, shoes, purse, whatever she wants. A whole weekend for her."

"You will talk to her after the father-daughter dance?"

"Yes. After the dance." She wouldn't spoil her daughter's fun. Olivia was sure Luc would be a father to be proud of, a welcome contrast to Jeremy, when Melissa found out about her natural father.

The session was over. Olivia stood to leave and stole a glance at Luc's handsome face while he scribbled on his pad. A dark strand of hair curled on his forehead when he bent his head. Yes, a father to be proud of. And a husband to...

The white shirt draped across his broad shoulders, stretching over the firm pecs. She licked her lips and suppressed the urge to touch and rub and feel.

He raised his head, his gaze straying toward her. Hunger simmered in his eyes.

She took a step forward.

"We are done for today." He averted his gaze, gathered his papers, and turned toward the door with a grunt.

Was he avoiding her? Now, when she wanted him so badly?

No way. She had to do something. Fast.

Tomorrow she'd call the school and volunteer her help during the father-daughter dance. And while buying things for Melissa, she'd choose a sophisticated dress for herself.

She wanted to share Melissa's fun but wouldn't tell Luc. An expert at keeping secrets, she lowered her lashes to hide her new longing and hoped he'd enjoy her surprise.

Be honest. What do you really want?

To be around Luc.

To feel and act like an attractive woman in a non-professional setting.

Could she lure him back to the idea of love, commitment and marriage?

Chapter Eleven

Today is the day.

Luc smacked his fist against his palm several times. He'd been preparing for Jeremy's interview for the last ten days. He'd read similar cases, studied different patients' symptoms, diagnoses and treatments, and was pretty sure he'd numbed any personal feelings. He checked the clock on the wall. Jeremy would be here in an hour. One last thing to do, notify Olivia to stay out of the way.

Luc reached for the phone, then thought better of it. He'd go to her office and tell her about Jeremy's appointment for this afternoon. He hadn't seen her today and missed her presence.

What was the matter with him?

Why would he seek her today when he'd made every effort to avoid her for the past week? He needed some space to sort out his feelings and understand hers before he could come up with a decision concerning a possible relationship.

He'd thought it would be easy enough to stay away from her with both of them extremely busy since McMillan's departure. Oddly enough, he'd bumped into her in every corner of the building, as if she'd done it on purpose to test his self-control.

Last week, when he drove away from her apartment, he'd come to the conclusion that Olivia was not a person he could play games with. Now, he was tired of quelling his feelings, frustrated at reining his lust and supremely upset at himself for his stupid suggestion of a fling.

A fling. To think of it, he really hated this word.

He strolled to the end of the hallway and knocked on her door.

"Come in."

He walked in and stopped in front of her desk. Olivia was working on her computer, just like the first time he'd seen her in her office. She stood, came toward him and dazzled him with a lovely smile.

"Luc, a pleasure to see you. You've been practically invisible this past week."

"*Bonjour*." Was it his imagination? Her eyes seemed brighter, their almond shape accentuated by a skillful dark line, her eyelids painted in light green. Had she been using mascara before? He'd never paid attention. Today she was a knockout, with a brush of pink on her cheeks and moist lipstick on her mouth.

And she wore a dress. A fluffy silk dress that skimmed her knees and fluttered around her legs. The moss green color enhanced the golden streaks of her hair.

"I...I..." Coming here was not a good idea after all.

Olivia waited for him to continue his sentence. Smiling and serene, and not helping at all. He had to say something. He looked at the wall for inspiration and noticed a silver frame. She'd kept his first gift all this time, hanging right in front of her desk. His blood raced a little faster. "You still have the painting of the Eiffel Tower?"

"It's been here for years."

How had he missed it the two times he'd come to her office? *Easily*. The first time he had eyes only for Olivia after such a long separation, and the second time he'd been struck by Melissa's resemblance to Jeremy.

"It's so pretty, isn't it?" She smiled coyly. "I wanted something French in my office. A reminder of my French boyfriend."

Luc swallowed hard. His Adam's apple somersaulted in his throat and knocked the air out of his lungs. If he didn't know better, he'd swear she was flirting with him. He perched his hip against the desk and laid his hand on it as he shook free of the ludicrous thought. The word flirt didn't exist in Olivia's vocabulary. Not the Olivia he knew ten years ago, and even less the one he'd found now when he returned.

"It is very pretty." *Mon Dieu*, she was the one *à croquer*. Pretty, good enough to eat. "Your dress is...*trés jolie*."

Merde. He'd stuttered. Him? The suave Frenchman accomplished at flattering women with twirling sentences.

"Thank you." Olivia stepped closer and put her hand on his.

His whole body hardened.

Good thing the mothers were not invited to the dance. Olivia in an evening dress would tempt a saint out of chastity. And Luc's recent chastity weighed heavily on his senses.

He needed Olivia. Body, mind and soul. He stared at her hand, cradled it and sucked in a deep breath, before releasing her. Now was the wrong time to play with fire.

He rammed his hands into his pockets and straightened, recalling his self-control *stat*.

"I came to tell you that I will meet with Jeremy at three o'clock."

Olivia's hand flew to her throat. She sobered up, her lovely smile wiped off her face at the imminence of the dreadful meeting. Her lower lip puckered, covering the upper one as she opened wide eyes. A mix of fear, anger and insecurity seethed in her aqua gaze. "I better leave right away. Before..." She lowered her eyelids. "I'm picking up Melissa and we're going shopping. Thank you for taking care of this."

He hated himself for spoiling her joyful mood.

"Have fun. Give Melissa a hug from me."

"I will." She gathered her purse in haste, yanked her raincoat from the coat rack and opened the door. He followed her and waited for her to lock her office.

"Everything will be fine."

She didn't answer. He walked her to the main door of the building, wondering if she'd even heard his reassuring words, then he stopped by his office to collect Jeremy's file before heading to the Crisis Center. He settled in the consultation room and waited for his new patient—the curse of Olivia's life.

****

By three fifteen, Luc shrugged and stood. He wasn't going to worry if Jeremy was a no-show today. Just as he made up his mind not to waste more time, the door opened.

Jeremy Rutherford entered. Head high, a confident smile on his face, the man walked in as if he were visiting an old acquaintance and extended his hand. "Jeremy Rutherford. Dr. Lucien, a pleasure to meet you."

Luc shook his hand and shoved away the thought that he was dealing with the man responsible for Olivia's misery. He surveyed Jeremy with an inquisitive look. "Please, have a seat."

Dressed in an expensive polo shirt, tailored slacks, and shiny black loafers, Jeremy was handsome, well built, a sportsman for sure, the type women fell for at first sight. No one could mistake him for a patient. But Luc had seen it all.

Jeremy sank in the chair and folded his left leg over his right knee. "I'm here only to please my grandfather. To be honest he's the one who should have his head examined. But he's eighty-five. I guess it's considered normal to become senile at that age." Jeremy threw his head backward and burst out laughing.

Luke ignored the unsavory joke and raucous laughter. “My understanding is you need a diagnosis to be cleared of abuse charges.”

Jeremy flipped the air with his hand. “Not to worry. I have the best lawyers for that.”

Luc extracted a printed form from under his pad and handed it to Jeremy with a pen. “We need you to sign here.”

“What’s this?”

“Your consent for evaluation and therapy. I can go through it with you if you want.”

Jeremy tapped his palm on the desk. “Hey, I’m here just because the old man threatened to cut me out of his will. You can evaluate all you want, but I’m not going through lengthy therapy. I’m saner than you are.” His mouth twitched as he sneered. He lowered his leg and scraped his shoes against the carpet with a rasping noise that grated on Luc’s ears.

“I can’t start this session without your signature.” Resting his elbows on the arms of the chair, Luc clenched his fingers and feigned indifference. He’d be delighted if Jeremy decided to leave.

“You’re wasting my time,” Jeremy bellowed, his smooth veneer melting away under pressure.

“Likewise,” Luc said, his voice impassive. “You can leave anytime, sir.”

“Hey, you know I can’t. I need my grandfather’s money.”

The grandfather had been right. Money, the ultimate stimulant for good behavior, would keep Jeremy here. Luc nodded. “These are official procedures.”

“Fine. Give me the damn paper.” He scribbled his name without reading the terms and conditions. “Go ahead, start.”

"What prompted you to come here, Mr. Rutherford?" Luc drew little lines on the pad to while away the time and keep his patience in check.

"I told you." Jeremy exhaled loudly. "The old man..."

"What events triggered Mr. Rutherford to ask you to come to us?" Luc lowered his eyes for a glimpse at his watch. At this rate he'd be here all night.

"Didn't he tell you?" Jeremy was determined to be difficult.

Luc suppressed a sigh and shook his head. This was going to be a continuous battle if Jeremy didn't cooperate. "Only what you tell me counts. I am not interested in the stories of other people."

"So you're going to believe only what I say." Jeremy smirked. "Hey, I like that. Okay, here's my story. The usual." He rotated his ruby ring around his finger. "I met this woman, Greta. A Swedish beauty. Great shape. Legs to die for. Blue eyes—"

"Just the events, please." Luc wrote *Greta* on his pad.

"We dated for a couple of years. I treated her nicely. Gave her everything she could dream of. She was happy with me. But what d'you know. The little tramp became greedy, wanted more. She stopped taking her pill to trap me into marriage." He narrowed his eyes, anger gushing with his words. "And I don't like to be trapped."

"What did you do?" Luc asked as he jotted a single word again, *trap*.

Jeremy shrugged. "I got angry, of course."

"And what did you do?"

"Well what do you expect an angry man to do when he's very upset?"

"Tell me exactly what happened." *Upset.* Another word to add on the pad.

"If you insist. But I warn you. This is

confidential. You can't go to the cops with this information."

"Everything you say here is confidential. I am your doctor."

"Good. So I got upset. I slapped her and told her to get an abortion. I was good enough to give her the address of a doctor who'd helped a few friends before. She argued we should keep the baby and get married. The trap."

Luc's throat constricted. It was almost Olivia's story unfolding.

"You see what I mean. I got very upset, and beat the hell out of her to teach her a lesson. The next day I discovered she'd run away. With my money." He flipped his hand. "I didn't care about the money, as long as I didn't see her again. The bitch went to the police. Can you imagine she filed a complaint against me, after I'd pampered her for two years?"

"Have you ever thought about having a child, Jeremy?" Luc squinted at his patient as he waited for the answer. How would Jeremy feel if he discovered he had a daughter now?

"What would I do with a child? It can be such a nuisance. My parents were never around to take care of me. I was raised by nannies. None of them stayed long."

Hmm, would that explain Jeremy's behavior? Luc scribbled *raised by nannies.*

"Do you resent your parents?"

"Of course, I do. People shouldn't have children if they can't stick around to take care of them. Maybe one day I'll change my mind and have a child. But when I decide."

Was it all about control as far as Jeremy was concerned?

"Have you ever thought about marriage?"

"Yes. I dated married women along the way. A different fun."

"Oh." Luc frowned. That wasn't what he'd meant with his question, but he played along to learn more about his patient. "Did you consider it a challenge?"

"Somehow. It was fun to get a woman to dump her husband or fiancé for me."

Fun. Challenge. Two more words reported on Luc's pad. "Have you ever considered getting married?" he asked, clarifying his original question.

"Sure. I did. But I like to be the one doing the asking. The one or two women I could have asked left me before I had time to seriously consider marriage."

"Do you think of marriage as a permanent relationship?"

"Permanent?" Jeremy sneered. "Doctor, you are naïve for a Frenchy. Why d'you think God invented divorce?"

Luc arched his eyebrow but didn't comment. "These two women you would have considered as prospective wives, why did they leave?"

Jeremy shrugged. "An argument. A fight."

"Did you hit them?"

"Yep." He raked his fingers through his hair. "Can't remember exactly why. They must have upset me."

"Did you throw them out?"

"Lord, no. I loved Laurie. I couldn't get enough of her body. But she left me."

"You didn't try to find her?"

"Of course, I did. I hired a detective. He found her for me. I went to see her. She didn't want to hear about coming back."

"And?"

"I got upset and I hit her."

"So you are usually calm and good to your women, but when you get upset you hit them." Definitely control issues.

"Exactly." Jeremy smacked the desk and smiled.

"Doctor, I'm glad you understand me so well."

"We have talked enough for today, Mr. Rutherford. We will continue the discussion next week." The hour of consultation was finally over.

"Well, that wasn't too bad. Glad you agree with me. If I have questions before my next appointment, I will drop by."

"No, you can't do that. I may be busy with other patients. We will discuss any questions you may have during our next session."

"What if I want to talk to you before that?"

Luc handed him a card. "You can call this number. The receptionist will give me your message, and I will call you back."

"I hope you'll answer right away," Jeremy said in a clipped tone. "I'm not a patient man."

"Mr. Rutherford, I will do my best to get back to you as soon as I can." Luc struggled to suppress his annoyance as he ushered Jeremy to the door. "Have a good evening."

"See you next week, doctor."

Luc breathed with relief when the door finally closed behind Jeremy. The arrogant bastard hadn't shown an ounce of remorse for mistreating his former girlfriends. Good thing Olivia had refused to treat Jeremy. Luc didn't doubt that Jeremy would consider her a nice challenge and try to lure her into his bed again, if only because he liked to coerce his women into submission.

After collecting his pad, Luc strode out of the Crisis Center. On his way to his office, he stopped at the cafeteria for a cup of coffee, then spent an hour typing on his laptop a detailed report based on the few words he'd jotted on his pad during the interview.

By six o'clock he headed home to the McMillan's mansion, his mind shut to everything but the father-daughter dance of tomorrow evening. Tonight after a good shower, he'd put some CDs on and practice his dance steps.

He wanted Melissa to be proud of her temporary father.

Chapter Twelve

"Can someone get the door?" Olivia called from the top of the stairs.

"Sure." Both the teenager and her grandmother answered at the same time. Melissa glided across the marble floor of the foyer toward the front door, her burgundy velvet dress swaying around her knees. A pair of patent, two-inch heel shoes dangling from one hand, she opened the door.

"Oh my God." Hearing her daughter's squeal, Olivia leaned over the banister. She had trouble stifling her own gasp as Luc walked in, hugged Melissa and strolled into the parlor to kiss Mama on both cheeks. He was drop-dead gorgeous. A sight to behold in a black tux and pristine white shirt highlighted with a satin bowtie. She couldn't afford to fail the elegance test.

Olivia looked down at her black silk dress, the epitome of discreet fashion, according to the sales clerk at Saks Fifth Avenue. It ought to be, considering its outrageous price, but it was so simple with its plunging V-neck, elbow-length sleeves, and straight narrow skirt. Olivia was glad she'd worn the pearl necklace and earrings her parents had given her for her med school graduation.

"You look stunning, my dear Luc. Absolutely dazzling." Marianna had no qualms lavishing her favorite man with compliments. For a change, she was right. "Melissa, you lucky girl, you'll have the most handsome man twirling you around."

"Mom," Melissa called toward the stairs as she slipped on her pumps. "Come on. I don't want to be late."

Luc raised his head. She'd expected him to chuckle or grin when he caught sight of her riveted in place, gawking at him. Instead, his eyebrows shot up, and he stared. She clutched her purse and shawl with one hand and the rail with the other.

As she started down the stairs, his eyes darkened, hot and sultry. His gaze roamed over her décolletage, skimmed her waist and slid along her legs encased in smoky pantyhose. Warm tingles spiraled from her throat down to her belly and her thighs.

Coming forward he extended his hand, palm open to help her down the last step, and bowed to brush a kiss on her knuckles. Her heart jolted.

"*Bonsoir*, Olivia." He looked at her, a question in his eyes.

"Good evening, Luc. I'm going to the dance as a chaperone." Olivia self-consciously touched her hair, wondered if her makeup were too obvious and fiddled with her shawl.

"Fantastic." His gaze drifted to her face, eyes glittering with a new fire as he smiled. "Lovely dress." His voice dropped to a whisper. "You look ravishing."

Goosebumps dotted her skin at his appreciative stare.

He took the shawl from her hands, spread it over her shoulders and smoothed it slowly down her back, his fingers warmer than the wool of her wrap. Heat seeped into her bones, and her knees weakened.

"Thank you." She wiggled free of his grasp and stepped forward.

Things were not going as anticipated. In her plan, *she* was supposed to conduct the seduction with a cool head and bring *him* back to the idea of marriage.

"I will be the luckiest man tonight with two beautiful ladies at my side." Luc presented both arms.

Melissa picked up her coat from the back of a chair and daintily hooked her fingers around his elbow. Olivia hesitated, then threw him a lopsided grin and followed suit.

"Have fun." Marianne stood at the door, beaming, a chocolate in her hand.

"Goodnight, Mom. Stop eating chocolate. Remember your cholesterol."

"*Bonne nuit*, Marianne."

"Night, Nana."

"There's no Cinderella curfew here. Take your time," her mother said as she waved them on their way.

"We won't be too late. I have to drive to my place tonight. I'm on call tomorrow and can't afford to be far in case the hospital calls."

Luc pressed her arm tighter against him. "Do not worry. I will drive you. It is a long way."

Marianna nodded. "Luc dear, it's a great idea to drive Olivia tonight. I'd be worried about her that late on the road."

"Mom! What are you talking about? I'm used to driving at any time of the day or night."

A wicked glint flashed in Marianna's eyes as she dismissed Olivia with a flip of her hand. "Luc, you come to dinner on Sunday. I'll make cannelloni with spinach for you and a duck *à l'orange*, dear."

"My favorite. I will be here for sure. Thank you, Marianna."

"Come on," Melissa called from the driveway. "I don't want to be the last one to get there."

"I can't believe it." Olivia slapped her purse against her thigh as Luc led her toward Doc's Mercedes, a hand at her back. "The woman is determined to push me into your arms."

"Yes?"

She caught Luc's wolfish smile and bit her tongue. She'd bet he was imagining a vivid picture of her literally falling into his arms. He cleared his throat. "Melissa is getting impatient."

Luc helped her in the car and shut the door after Melissa. "Where should I go, ladies?"

"Turn right out of the driveway, left at the second light, then straight for five minutes," Melissa instructed. "You'll see the high school on your right."

When they arrived, Luc dropped them at the entrance and went to park. They waited for him in the school lobby. A couple of girls joined them with their dads in tow.

Melissa bent toward Olivia and whispered, "Mom, see this girl in pink? She's the one whose mother is French." Raising her voice, she introduced her friend. "Christine will be going to France with me. She gave me those French magazines her mother receives to browse through."

Olivia smiled at the pretty teenager. Actually, all the girls looked lovely in their finery, neatly set hair and light makeup. But my baby is one of the prettiest, Olivia thought with motherly pride as she admired her daughter.

Melissa turned toward her friend, her mane of blond hair floating around her shoulders. "Wait till you see the guy who's my father tonight. A knock-out."

Melissa was right. Although he seemed unaware of his charm, Luc could be a heartbreaker. Good thing the female crowd was under seventeen. Olivia didn't want competition around as she launched into a thorough campaign to win Luc's heart again. For good.

He came back and escorted them inside the gymnasium transformed into a glitzy ballroom for the joyful occasion.

"It looks like a wedding reception." Melissa couldn't contain her glee. The cafeteria tables dressed with full-length pink tablecloths and the white-covered chairs tied with pink organdy ribbons had completely transformed the huge room. Melissa pointed to the basketball nets concealed under clusters of balloons.

"We'll drop them at midnight." Olivia mentally patted herself on the back for taking the time to study the schedule of events. "Now, I'd better start my duties." She slid into her seat at a table lined with cards printed in black with a calligraphy number. She handed Luc one. "Here's yours. Table five. You're right on the dance floor."

People filed in to get their seating arrangements, and Olivia stopped paying attention to her daughter and companion.

"May I get you a drink?" Luc asked, from behind her.

"They're serving fruit punch and soft drinks tonight." Olivia stifled a smile, wondering how her Frenchman would survive without wine.

"Punch is perfect. Come, Melissa." He took her daughter's arm.

Olivia followed them with a tender smile as they negotiated their way to the makeshift bar, received their drinks and returned with three glasses of punch filled to the brim.

"Mom, this one's for you."

"Thanks. Go have fun." She smiled, then attended to the other guests.

Suddenly the lights flickered and dimmed. Dance music blasted through the room. To Olivia's amazement, Luc pulled Melissa out of her chair. The first couple on the dance floor, they started swinging and shaking, soon followed by the crowd of girls and dads. An hour later, Melissa, laughing, her eyes bright, came toward her dragging Luc by the hand.

"Mom, I need a break. I can lend you my father for a dance."

Her father. Olivia's breath caught in her throat. If only it were true.

"I can't dance. I'm on duty. Besides, this soiree is only for the students and their fathers."

"Nope. See Jennifer's mom is dancing with her dad, and my class room teacher, Miss Brown, is dancing with the principal." Melissa took Olivia's hand and put it in Luc's large one. "Come on, Mom. Loosen up. Luc, go easy on Mom. I've never seen her dance. It's her first time."

"Melissa!"

Luc burst out laughing. "These children think their parents are ancient. Ready for a demonstration of my wonderful dance steps, Olivia?"

He pulled her to the dance floor just as rock music started. "Luc, I don't want to attract attention to us. Some of the staff are here, and they all know me as a serious doctor."

"So? You are entitled to have some fun." He wrapped an arm around her waist, swung to the strong beat of the music, spun her into his arms and out again. Olivia laughed and followed his fast-paced lead as they moved and grooved to the music. He was a good dancer, and she delighted at being in his arms. When the rock music stopped, she felt flushed and disappointed it had ended so quickly.

Luc held her hand, preventing her from going back to her table. "Everyone is seated. Melissa is eating her dinner and talking to her friends. We can dance a little longer."

Without waiting for her answer, he pulled her against him. As the band played a slow tune, they glided around with little steps. "Did I tell you how beautiful you look?"

She chuckled. "As a matter of fact you did."

"And you smell divine." His gaze drifted from

her eyes to her mouth, then veered off to the ballroom where hundreds of teenagers and their dads ate and danced. He exhaled. "I guess we have to behave."

"We'd better." She sighed and closed her eyes, then snapped them open as she, too, remembered the age of the crowd surrounding them.

Luc tightened his hold on her back. "Melissa was wrong. You dance very well."

"You too. Did you have a lot of practice in Paris?"

"Some. Although I would have rather been dancing with you," he whispered against her hair.

"I haven't seen you for ten years. No serious relationships during all that time?" She tilted her head, suddenly curious to learn everything about him, particularly his love life.

Luc captured her gaze and smiled. "None. I couldn't find a single woman comparable to you, *chérie*."

"Oh Luc, what a nice compliment." Her heart hummed with the band, and a happy feeling danced deep inside her as their gazes locked. At that moment she knew without a shadow of a doubt that she had never stopped loving him.

She wanted him now. She wanted him forever.

Hope fluttered in the air, but she couldn't stand the tension of being in his arms and not kissing him. If she'd so much as tip her face up, their lips would touch. Her cheeks flushed, and her fingers curled around the lapel of his jacket.

Stop looking at me.

When the music ended, Olivia glanced at the punch table. She was terribly thirsty but didn't want to inconvenience Luc with a request for a drink. "Be right back. Wait a second."

She sauntered to the table, ignored the two punch bowls and fetched a bottle of water. She poured herself a glass and drank half of it right away, then filled it again and carried it with her. When she walked back, Luc was conversing with one of the dads.

"Count Vicour-Michelet, what a surprise. I recognized you from your many pictures in the magazines. My wife was a college friend of Marie-Claire's," the dad said, his voice reaching Olivia in spite of the background noise of the room. "She showed me your pictures with Marie-Claire in *Paris-Match* and *Vogue*. Congratulations on your engagement, sir."

Olivia stopped in her tracks. The man's last word squeezed her heart like a pair of medical tweezers. Luc glanced at her from above the man's shoulder and frowned.

"*Enchanté*, Monsieur. Please excuse me." Luc edged around the man and ushered her away.

"I have to help with the desserts," she said, looking at the crowd.

"Olivia, please, do not pay attention to what he said. It is nothing."

"Luc, don't worry. I mean, I didn't even know you'd show up in Cincinnati again. It'd be ridiculous on my part to question your private life." She averted her eyes, unable to face him.

"Still, I want to explain." His hand on her back, he led her to an empty table at the far corner of the ballroom, out of earshot.

"Marie-Claire?" The name stung, but she shrugged. "You don't owe me any explanations. Remember you wanted simple fun between us. That's it."

That was not it. He had kissed her on three occasions, and she had hoped that tonight... Empty dreams. She slumped into a chair. Her insides twisted. Her blood roiled.

"Marie-Claire was nothing more than a

companion for a few outings."

"Sure. But I don't believe a man can go that long without women." She bit her tongue as soon as she blurted it. What an idiotic thing to say.

His eyebrow arched. "I never pretended I remained celibate for ten years."

She blushed furiously. Did he have to be so blunt? Damn his honesty. "I understand."

"No, you do not." The left side of his mouth twitched slightly. He sat beside her. "Listen, Olivia. The paparazzi reported regularly about my public appearances. It is all gossip, trash. The bold ones announced my engagement twice a year to the latest lady hanging onto my arm." He raised his hands and then clasped them together. "And I disappointed them regularly."

"I see. The Count de Vicour-Michelet fed the gossip column with his many conquests." So, he was a big shot in the social arena as well as the medical field. She couldn't care less about the latest lady hanging on his arm, or the one before her.

She surveyed the room, trying to ignore the painful stab nudging her side. Jealousy? *Never*.

"You should go finish your dinner before it gets cold," she said, her voice icy enough to freeze any meal. "I'm going to check if they need me at the buffet."

"I will walk you to the buffet table."

"No need." She turned away, leaving him staring at her, and strode toward the wall where the long table adorned with various platters of food was slowly being depleted. She helped clear the table and set the dessert.

Her task finished, Olivia darted her gaze toward the dance floor. Luc and her daughter participated in a dance competition now. She hoped they'd win. Studying their performance, she was sure they would. Luc always won, always topped those around him. No wonder the women loved him.

He'd mentioned his social life as if he were reporting casual facts or uninteresting events, but the information dampened her fun. A hotshot count with an aristocratic name, even if he practiced medicine, was out of her league. She missed her Luc, the dazzling resident she'd loved.

Did he still exist, outside her dreams?

Now she was dealing with a successful doctor and a count. The ladies' adulation and the press interest must have changed him. Good grief, by his own admission the man couldn't go out without a woman hanging on his arm, an extra beautiful ornament to enhance his sex appeal.

Olivia would probably be an amusing interlude for him. No wonder he suggested some no-strings-attached fun. Unless she just attracted his attention as another case to treat, one to add to his successful medical record.

Frustration simmered in her gut. She tried to ignore it and busied herself by handing out the desserts. A grumbling in her stomach reminded her she hadn't eaten anything since lunch. She helped herself to a slice of German chocolate torte, finished it and scooped some chocolate mousse. After she licked her fork, she reached for a triangle of black forest cheesecake.

Chocolate, the universal anti-anxiety remedy, according to her mother. Too bad Olivia couldn't prescribe it to her patients.

"Are you worshipping a chocolate god tonight?" She dropped her fork as Luc's laughter pierced through her bitter thoughts.

"I realized I'd forgotten to eat."

"I will get you something from the kitchen."

"No. I'm not hungry anymore. Soon they'll drop the balloons, and we can leave." She reached for a glass of punch to cool her throat. She shouldn't have stuffed herself with chocolate. It sat like a heavy stone inside her stomach.

Indigestion is one of the symptoms of anxiety.

But she wasn't anxious or worried or frustrated. Not at all. She just wanted to scratch out his eyes and run away like a stupid teenager crying over her first crush.

He gave her a questioning look. "Are you tired? Why don't you come and sit at our table. There are places. A girl and her father already left."

At that moment, a woman announced on the microphone, "The winning couple for the best performance in our dancing competition is: Melissa Crane and her dad. Please come forward for your prize."

"Hey, we won." Luc clapped his hands.

Olivia couldn't help smiling at his boyish enthusiasm.

Melissa's dad. Oh God, if only it were true.

Tears of frustration stung Olivia's eyes, and her cheeks felt about ten degrees too warm. She cleared her throat and blinked. "Go, go. Melissa is looking for you." With her hand she urged him away, her bitterness forgotten for the moment.

"You come with me." He grabbed her hand and dragged her behind him toward the end of the dance floor where her daughter waited for them, a huge smile brightening her face.

The coordinator opened a jewelry box to reveal a silver chain and porcelain rose pendant. She gave it to Melissa and handed a similar box with a keychain to Luc. "Congratulations to our winning couple."

Displaying her pendant, Melissa smiled from ear to ear. "Mom, it was fantastic. I never had so much fun in my life." She turned toward Luc and threw her arms around his neck. "Thank you, Luc. I wish you could be my dad for real."

Liquid sloshed on the floor as Olivia almost

dropped the punch glass she held with a shaking hand.

"And I, too, wish I could be your dad for real." Luc hugged Melissa. Over her shoulder, his eyes bored into Olivia's. "You are very special to me."

Olivia's breath caught up in her throat.

Was he talking to her?

How special, Count de Vicour-Michelet?

Chapter Thirteen

Luc dropped Melissa at the house, but captured Olivia's hand when she tried to follow her daughter out of the car. "Stay."

She raised a stubborn chin. "I said I can drive myself. I don't need a chauffeur."

"I flatter myself that I care about you more than a chauffeur. You are on call tomorrow, and it's midnight. No need to exhaust yourself with a long drive. Besides, I have something to tell you."

"I'm too tired to talk."

"Then take a nap. I will be as quiet as a mouse."

She pulled her hand away and released an exaggerated sigh. "You can be really exasperating."

"I know, but I still insist on driving you to your apartment."

Olivia threw a look at the darkened house. Melissa was already inside and had closed the door behind her. And sure enough, Marianna had switched the lights off to signify she wasn't expecting Olivia back inside.

"My car is here."

"You will come back with me on Sunday for dinner and drive it back."

"And if I'm called tomorrow, I'll have to take a taxi?"

"I'll pick you up tomorrow morning. I have work to do anyway."

She huffed a couple of times and crossed her arms. "Okay, there's no need to spend the night arguing in my mother's driveway."

He took off smoothly, inserted a CD of Celine

Dion's love songs and remained silent to allow her to rest, but he promised himself he would clarify the misunderstanding as soon as they reached her place. Tonight. Before she made a mountain out of a molehill.

Of all the bad luck. To meet someone who knew Marie-Claire. As if he gave a damn about Marie-Claire or Sophie or...he'd already forgotten some of the names. Well, he wasn't being fair to Marie-Claire. She was a stunning beauty and a successful lawyer, not a gold digger like the others.

A tapping of fingers on the seat belt attracted his attention. Olivia hadn't slept after all.

"Are you still upset?" he asked with his softest voice and turned off the CD player. He'd better clear the air right away.

"Upset? What about?" Her voice sliced through the air like a newly sharpened scalpel. "It was a great party and my daughter is happy. That's all that matters to me."

"Yes, I know. But I have not been totally honest in my explanation earlier. It bothers me."

"Oh." That had her attention. "What do you mean?"

"About Marie-Claire. She has been more than just a date."

Olivia swiveled her head toward him, her eyes flashing darts in the semi-darkness of the car. "I see."

"She is the daughter of my mother's best friend. I knew her when we were kids."

"Spare me the details. I'm not your shrink. And I'm really not interested." She hissed as she turned her head toward the passenger window.

"But I need to explain the truth."

"Yeah? The sacrosanct truth you worship but ignore when it suits you." She spat the words with such rage Luc thought she'd punch him with the next sentence.

"The truth is my mother kept nagging me about getting married and having a child."

"Sure. The Count de Vicour-Michelet needs an heir."

"Exactly. My mother brought us together. I took Marie-Claire out several times during the next six months."

"And you slept with her." She gasped and folded her hands in her lap. "I'm sorry, I can't believe I said that."

"I slept with her. And I bought a ring."

"Ha. Enough." The headlights of an oncoming car flickered over her furrowed forehead and pursed lips. "You, bastard, you kissed me while you are engaged to another woman."

He let go of the insult he didn't deserve. "I am not engaged. I received McMillan's e-mail telling me you read my articles and recommended me the day before I was supposed to propose. Instead of proposing, I returned the ring and took Marie-Claire out as planned, but I told her I was leaving for the U.S."

"And you broke her heart, you selfish bastard."

Again? An insult because he almost proposed to another woman and an insult because he hadn't. There was no way to please Olivia. It wasn't like her to lose control of her civility. A proof she was shaken, upset, and hopefully jealous.

"No, I did not." He held her gaze for a moment, wanting her to absorb what he'd reveal next, even though her culture differed from his French traditions. "Our marriage was going to be one of convenience. It is often done in French society. She did not love me, and she knew I did not love her. She also knew she had to deliver a child in exchange for the security of my name and the title of countess. And each of us would keep our freedom."

"But—I can't believe what I'm hearing. You'd cheat on each other?"

"There would have been no cheating and no love. Only honesty, friendship, and understanding. Marie-Claire hugged me before I left and wished me good luck. She knew everything about my American girlfriend from ten years ago. My only girlfriend."

He wouldn't tell Olivia more now and give her the upper hand to trash his heart again. But her gasp was sweet music to his ear. He had finally cracked her wall of cool reserve.

"You talked to...to this woman about me? Ten years after you left Cincinnati?"

"Actually, I talked about you to every woman I took out more than a few times."

"Why? To protect your independence and keep the prospective brides at bay?"

He laughed. It was typical of Olivia to look at the practical side rather than the sentimental. "In a way, yes."

She smiled for the first time since she'd heard about Marie-Claire. "In that case you owe me big time. I saved your neck from the for-better-or-worse noose."

They'd reached her building. He parked his car in a visitor's spot and turned toward her. "Yes, I owe you, and I intend to thank you." He cradled her shoulders, pulled her toward him and folded her into his arms, before she had the time to react.

"Hey, what do you think you're doing?" She jerked her head backward and squirmed to free herself.

He tightened his hold on her back and chuckled, his lips a mere inch from her mouth. "Thank you with a kiss." Not a soft and timid kiss. He was done walking on eggshells around her. This time he wanted to brand her with his kiss. He wanted her to remember it as long as she lived.

He closed the space between them and lowered his head, molding his lips to hers until she relaxed in his hold. His tongue outlined the curves of her mouth, demanding an invitation.

Her moan fired his blood up another notch. When her lips parted, he invaded her mouth, tasted chocolate, and played, and stroked.

And she finally responded, sucking his tongue and performing a wild dance around it with her own. Her warm and pliant body leaned into his, and her perfume enveloped him. Strong and heady. Jasmine and orange. Her fingers linked behind his neck. Her breasts pressed against his chest. He inched his fingers between their bodies and gently fondled.

It was stupid to start this in the car, in a parking lot. He released her mouth and feathered kisses along her cheek.

"*Chérie*, please let's not torture each other. We have wasted ten years." He sucked in a deep breath and eased away.

"Ten years," Olivia repeated, in a whisper. He was right. *Ten years wasted.* She had yearned for him every single day during those ten long years while he apparently talked about her to his many French girlfriends.

No, not girlfriends. Dates or escorts.

He said she'd been his only girlfriend. She believed him. Luc never lied. And she wanted him as much as he wanted her.

Now. Right away.

And tomorrow? What would happen tomorrow? "The hell with tomorrow." She realized too late she'd voiced her frustration.

"We should live in the present," he whispered against her mouth and kissed her again with the passion she'd never forgotten.

When she managed to breathe, she cradled his cheeks in her hands and smiled. "Can I invite you upstairs for a drink?"

His gaze locked on hers, peering into her soul. "Have I convinced you? Do you really want me to come?"

"I really want you." She sealed her words with a kiss on his lips.

"In that case, I could use a Cognac." He stroked her hair and offered her a dazzling smile before opening the car door and walking her to her apartment.

She felt strong, confident, elated with his arm around her waist. Anticipation warmed her belly with spiraling flames. She'd been waiting for this moment for ten long years.

When they entered her apartment, she switched the lights on and closed the door behind them. "Make yourself comfortable," she said as she kicked off her high-heeled pumps.

Luc removed his jacket and bowtie, and undid the top button of his shirt. He looked around him, surveying the living room. "Nice place you have here. It is exactly as I expected, neat, elegant and cozy." He pointed to a Monet painting above the white leather couch. "And you put in a French touch."

"Always. I can't live without the French touch."

He grinned and strolled toward the credenza that served as a buffet and a bar.

"Is there anything else we need to talk about? I mean about your many lady friends," she said as he poured two drinks with as much ease as if he lived in this apartment.

"*Non*. No more mention of other women. But I can talk about you all night long and never be bored." He gave her a glass and clicked his against hers. "*A la tienne*. To you."

"Cheers."

He swirled the golden liquid, brought it to his

nose and inhaled. "*C'est bon*. Very good." He drained it and refilled it for himself. "Do you remember our last time together?"

"The time you told me you were leaving?"

"And you told me you never wanted to see me again because your career was more important than empty feelings. No. That's a day I have tried hard to forget. I was talking about the last time we...hmm...made love."

"Oh." Heat crept up her neck and face.

"We came back from your graduation party straight to your little student apartment. You wore a black silk dress like tonight and this pearl necklace. Your hair was floating down your back. We had a glass of Chardonnay."

She brought her hand to her throat. God, he hadn't forgotten any details. "I-I remember."

"You gave me a soft kiss."

"As usual you changed it into a torrid one."

He came toward her, seized her hand and led her to the couch. "And do you remember I pulled you onto my lap, just like now." He dropped onto the leather sofa and dragged her down with him. His hands trailed up her arms, skimmed her shoulders. The feather-like caress strayed to her throat, sending a tingle of pleasure all the way to her belly.

And here she thought she'd never sit on his lap again. She basked in the intimacy of their position. "I remember the scent of your cologne, amber and spice." Closing her eyes, she nuzzled his neck and inhaled. "The same as you have on today."

"Oh my darling." Cupping her face between his palms, he captured her mouth in a deep kiss that left her breathless. When he released her, he smiled, and his eyes twinkled with merriment. "Let's remember more things. I unclasped your necklace, and then I unzipped your dress. Like this." He removed her jewelry, lowered her bodice down her arms and exposed her black lace bra.

"And then—" He swiftly unclasped her bra and eased it away. His gaze flickered from one breast to the other, warming her with anticipated pleasure. "Gorgeous," he whispered as he raised his eyes.

Raw desire blazed in their blue depth and mirrored her own excitement.

Mesmerized, she hooked her arms around his neck, snuggled against his chest and breathed the masculine smell that made her dizzy with want.

"And then... Like this?" She smiled, ready to give as good as she got. "Your shirt has to go." The buttons snapped open to reveal the muscular chest she'd recalled more than once in her fantasies. "Beautiful."

He chuckled when she mimicked his words and moves, and, with a swift motion he threw his shirt away, but when she contoured his nipples with her tongue, he stiffened, his arousal pushing into her thigh.

"Where is your bedroom, *chérie*?"

She waved her head toward the right. "This way. We'll save the grand tour for later."

He pulled her to her feet. She glanced at her dress draped over her hips.

"Leave it," he rasped. "I like the black against your whiteness." His thumb played at the base of her throat, zigzagged to the valley between her breasts, dipped to her belly button where her creamy flesh vanished under dark silk.

Unable to withstand the fire created by his touch, she took his hand and led him to the bedroom. As she passed the mirror over her dresser, she gasped at their reflection. She looked like a Salomé dancer who'd shed her veils, leading the conqueror to her bed.

His eyes roamed her half nudity and the swaying of her breasts. Her conqueror licked his lips, and her mouth went dry. Could she suggest he lick her lips instead, or her breasts, or...?

She sighed.

He groaned.

The deep-throated sound stirred more hunger in her belly. She slipped away from him to switch on the night table lamp. When she turned around, her breasts brushed his chest. "Oh, you—" she murmured. She hadn't heard him pad behind her, but the grazing of her nipples over his rigid torso zipped a new surge of lust along her nerves.

His arms closed around her, stroked her lower back and settled on her hips. He fingered the material and smoothed her dress down her legs. She wriggled and shimmied out of it, eager to have no barrier of cloth between them. Without saving a glance to the heap on the floor, his gaze skated from her face to her breasts and belly. "Very sexy dress. Was it meant to seduce me?"

She tilted her head and chuckled. "Are you always the perceptive shrink?"

"*Chérie*, I am utterly seduced. But to be honest, you are more beautiful without it." His smile slowly faded as his fingers lead a maddening dance around her bikini panties. "*Mon Dieu*, you are even more beautiful than ten years ago."

He ripped his clothes off and flung them on a chair, his breathing heavy. She flipped her hair back, rubbed her neck and took a step forward, hypnotized by his rippling chest, flat belly, corded muscles tempting her to stroke and knead. She lowered her head...and encountered the bulge in his briefs.

What was he waiting for? She was on fire, hot, wet and ready. She licked her lips and opened her arms. "Love me, Luc."

He wrapped his arms around her, pressed her against the rigid length of his body. "I do, *mon amour*, I do," he whispered against hers lips.

He does? He does what exactly?

Her gasp was muffled under a searing kiss as he devoured her mouth. *Forget about questions now.* She tasted sweet alcohol on his tongue as it explored the recesses of her mouth. Old feelings came rushing over her in a decadent wave when he fondled her breast and squeezed her bottom.

A song hummed in her brain. *Feelings, feelings I don't recognize. Feelings I've been longing for.* She sucked on his tongue and returned his kiss with all her pent-up passion. He trailed his lips along her collarbone and around her breast, nibbled on one nipple and then on the other.

"Luc, please." She moaned as heat engulfed her.

He carried her to the bed, lowered her panties down her legs and lay down next to her. His hand slid between her thighs, and his fingers started a mind-boggling dance inside her. She splayed a hand over his shoulders, raked his back and pulled at his shoulders. "Luc, now, please."

His chest covered her upper body, hard muscles against soft flesh. She squirmed and flexed her hips to meet him.

"Soon, *chérie*." He'd always delayed his pleasure to enhance hers.

"Now," she ordered, frazzled by the sweet torture. She eased away, brushed her hand down his length and curled her fingers around his erection, gently rubbing it against herself.

"Not yet." He pulled away, fumbled in the pocket of his discarded pants and protected himself.

"You came ready for tonight?" Her voice drifted as she raised her head from the pillow to watch the magnificent male specimen displayed for her eyes only.

"I have been ready since I landed in Cincinnati. Why do you think I took this assignment?" He sat on the bed and traced his thumb along her jaw.

"You came all the way from France to sleep with me?" She wrinkled the sheet with nervous fingers, not knowing what to make of this confession.

"To see you, to be with you, to rekindle our... relationship." He chuckled. "And yes, to sleep with you, as a bonus."

"You came only for me? What about your research?"

"To hell with the research. Only for you, *mon amour*. The research was my official excuse." He reclined beside her and caressed her breasts with a slow and maddening motion and gently teased the hardened nipples. "Are you ready for me?"

"Oh Luc." Still unable to believe that maybe he loved her enough to forget the past and live in the present the way she wanted, she closed her eyes and linked her arms around his neck.

He rolled on top of her and entered her slowly. The heat that started in her belly spread in a whirling sensation through her body. She wrapped her legs around him and pressed her hips high against him. He pulled out and pushed back in, rocking himself inside her.

"Olivia," he murmured as he pumped hard into her softness.

A rainbow of colors splashed behind her eyelids and hundred of stars exploded in magnificent fireworks. She kneaded his butt and matched the tempo of his thrust. When the fire inside her blazed to an all-time high, she dug her nails into his shoulders. "I love you," she whispered and raised her head to meet his kiss.

"*Je t'aime, mon amou*r." He breathed the words into her mouth as he fused his body to hers and shuddered.

****

Luc woke to the faint rays of sunshine filtering

through the Venetian blinds. The soft form nestled against him squirmed and snuggled closer to his side. He tried to remain perfectly still but a part of his lower anatomy rose to attention and poked against her belly. He smiled as she dug her head in the hollow of his collarbone.

She moaned, squinted and shut her eyelids as if she found the effort unbearable. And then she suddenly opened them wide, staring straight into his eyes.

He kissed the tip of her nose. "*Bonjour*. Did you have sweet dreams?"

"Hmm." Her dazed expression was answer enough. His beautiful siren couldn't extricate herself from her dreams. He anchored her against him with a hand on her back and captured her mouth under his. She hooked an arm around his neck and slithered a hand down toward his erection. "Hmm."

He chuckled. "If *hmm* means you want more, I am ready." He lifted her on top of him, cupped her lovely derriere in both hands and lowered her onto his shaft. She wriggled and matched his hunger, thrust for thrust, kisses mingled with moans.

They exploded together, and she collapsed on his chest, her nipples teasing his muscles, her heart beating in cadence with his own.

When he came back to earth, he stroked a soothing hand over her mussed hair. "*Bonjour, mon amour*."

She raised her head and swiped the beads of perspiration from his forehead with the tip of her finger. Her gaze sparkled with a dazzling aqua light.

"I can't believe it, Luc. It was...simply fantastic. Just like before."

"Better than before." He chuckled. "Perfect chemistry with no need for a catalyst." He cradled her cheeks and sobered. "Tell me, *chérie*, last night you said something in the throes of passion. You said, 'I love you, Luc.' Was it real or a moan of passion?"

"And you said the same in French. Is it true?" As usual, she was a master at evading personal questions. But he loved the feeling of her body sprawled on top of him in total abandon and he planned to keep her there for as long as he could.

"You know me better, *chérie.* I would never lie to you."

"When did you start loving me?" She raked her hand through his hair and curled a strand around a finger.

"I never stopped. Why do you think I never married in all these years?"

"You mean you already loved me back then? Seriously loved me?"

"Very seriously."

"But—?"

"When I started to be sentimental, you did your best to discourage me. 'My career is the most important thing in my life'. Does it sound familiar? You managed to spoil every one of our dates with this statement."

"Oh. It was because of Melissa."

"Yes, I realize that now." He agreed with her, but deep down he labeled her negative attitude as fear of commitment.

Was she still afraid of commitment, after the incredible chemistry they shared a moment ago?

She started rolling off him. "We'd better get dressed. I may get a call soon."

"Not yet, *chérie.*" She was so cute, naked and flushed, and talking business. He clamped a hand to her butt, keeping her welded to his length, and kissed her thoroughly. "Your turn. Did you mean what you said last night?"

He had satisfied her curiosity and would not let her off the hook so easily. *Mon Dieu*, she couldn't even guess how his chest had exploded with joy when he heard her speak of love. Finally, after waiting an eternity. Was it true?

She turned her head, tried to avoid his gaze. “Olivia, please. The truth only.”

“You heard it.”

He swallowed, not wanting to insist and see her withdraw behind a cold mask. Yet, he needed to know. “When did you start loving me?” He repeated her question.

She gave him the most beautiful smile he’d ever seen. “I loved you ten years ago and never stopped.”

For a second, he thought he’d heard it wrong. It couldn’t be. He raised himself against the headboard and pulled her onto his lap. This was too important to miss a word. “Ten years ago, you asked me to go away and never come back. Did you love me back then?”

In fascination, he watched her breasts rise and fall as she inhaled deeply and exhaled.

Concentrate on what she is saying.

She closed her eyes. “Yes, I did. Luc, I loved you from the first time I sat in your class and you asked me my name.”

“*Ma chérie, mon amour.*” He closed his arms around her and tucked her head against his shoulder. But then...

Silence fell between them as he analyzed her confession. She loved him ten years ago, but hadn’t hesitated to push him away because of Melissa.

What was different now?

Would she push him away again if he asked her for a commitment?

Probably.

As long as Melissa didn’t know the truth about her father, Olivia would live in fear, and sacrifice herself.

And sacrifice Luc in the process.

He'd had it with this situation, with the lies and the silence that had shut him out of her life.

He swore under his breath. Something had to change. Immediately.

Olivia had to talk to her daughter. Right away. Only then would she be ready to consider a future with him.

"Time to get dressed." He eased her away from him before he gave in to temptation again.

"Why are you scowling? I don't understand. What's wrong?" Her mouth pleated in disappointment. And he hated himself for causing it.

"We have a busy day. Hospital. And then dinner at your mother's. Olivia, now is the time to talk to Melissa. She's relaxed after the party and so are you."

She jumped out of bed. Without bothering to cover herself, she turned and glared at him. "Luc, you see why I never told you I love you. Because you're always so inflexible it scares the hell out of me."

He shoved a hand through his hair and blew out a frustrated breath. "Please, Olivia, do it now. I will be with you. Do it for Melissa, for yourself and for me."

She stared at him. A mix of emotions played in her eyes as he waited for her decision.

Would she give them a chance at happiness or slam the door in his face again?

Chapter Fourteen

Where had the morning gone? Olivia couldn't remember doing a single productive thing. Sitting in the consultation room of the Crisis Center, she smoothed her skirt to erase an invisible wrinkle. Luc had sat in with her for a new evaluation. Then they'd visited Hailey, the suicidal patient, who was doing much better and was about to be discharged from the hospital.

Luc came toward Olivia and rested his hands on her arms. "Do you want to take a break while I handle the next case?" He'd been at her side all day, his smile never wavering.

She shook her head. What kind of doctor would she be if she neglected her patients because of her personal problems? "I'm fine. Don't worry. I'll talk to Melissa. I won't chicken out anymore."

God, I hope I can do it. I hope it's the right thing.

"I never doubted your inner strength."

Puckering her mouth, she lowered her head. When it came to hurting her daughter, she'd play chicken without guilt. "You have more faith in me than I do." If he didn't stare at her with so much hope, and love, she'd be tempted to postpone her revelations to next week or next month.

He gave her shoulders a gentle squeeze and resumed his place as a nurse knocked on the door and craned her neck through the opening. "The Tarino family," she said. "All five of them," she added in a hushed voice.

Olivia caught sight of Luc's arched brow and shrugged, palms open. "It's supposed to be Teresa

Tarino only." She shot a wary look at the doorway. "Teresa?"

A short woman with a baby in her arms entered, flicking panicky glances around. A lanky man ambled past her. "I'm sorry Dr. Crane, but Emilio wanted to talk to you too, and I couldn't leave Holly and her little brothers alone," the woman said as she dropped onto a chair, the baby in her lap.

A teenage girl with heavy mascara around her eyes sauntered in, holding a toddler boy by the collar of his shirt. The consultation room filled with the smell of cheap perfume, escalating Olivia's stress into a full-blown headache.

"They ain't my brothers I told you a hundred times. And I ain't their nanny either." Holly pushed the little boy toward her mother and settled in the other chair.

Heaving a deep breath, Olivia shoved her own problem to the back of her mind and readied herself for a rough hour. "Teresa, it will be difficult to have a productive consultation with your whole family around."

Olivia flipped a look from her patient to the man standing next to her chair. How could she help the poor woman with the husband glaring at her and the daughter trying her best to be obnoxious?

"Emilio, I am Dr. Lucien. I am here to give a second opinion. Would you mind explaining your presence at your wife's psychiatric session?" Luc asked, not one bit intimidated by the man's scowl.

"I'm here because I'm fed up with seeing my wife lazing away all day long on a sofa. Can't you do something to make her more energetic?"

"Your wife was depressed after the baby's birth," Olivia explained. "You should be patient and help her. It takes time to get over postpartum depression." Especially if this husband kept lashing his wife with harsh criticism. This was an absolute waste of time. "I noticed she missed her appointment twice last month."

"Yeah, I didn't let her come. I don't believe in this depression baloney. Teresa's supposed to go to work and bring in some money. We can't continue like this. I'll take my baby and leave."

"Good riddance," the teenager muttered.

"Shut up," the man snarled while Teresa threw a hand up in supplication.

"Please don't leave us, Emilio. I'll go to work. I'll get better soon. Dr. Crane, can I double the dose of my medicine?"

"Absolutely not. You have to continue taking one capsule of *Cymbalta*. This antidepressant has a delayed-release action and will release 60 mg in your body during the course of a day. Any overdose can be extremely dangerous."

"So what am I going to do?" Teresa wrung her hands.

Obviously, Teresa would not get better in the type of environment she lived in. "I'll refer you to Social Services. They may be able to help."

"Thank you, doctor." Husband and wife answered together.

"I appreciate any help," Emilio said, his voice more subdued than when he came in. "I really want us to stay together as a family," the man added as he glanced at the teenager who blatantly turned her head. "I had so many hopes when we got married. If only things would improve."

"Emilio, would you mind stepping out for a moment with the small ones? I'd like to talk to Teresa and Holly," Olivia said, determined to get to the bottom of the situation. She had the nagging feeling the daughter was doing her best to upset her stepfather and add more stress to her mother.

"Why? So the girl can say nasty lies about me," Emilio asked with a we've-been-through-that look at

Holly.

"I'm your wife's doctor, and Dr. Luc is a world-famous psychiatrist. We, both, want to help your family. You said you hoped things could improve. Right?"

"Of course. I want to see things improve. I love my wife," he grumbled and cast a disgusted look at Holly.

"Well, let me talk to her. Can you step out for a few minutes?"

"If you think it can make a difference." Emilio took the baby and extended a hand to the toddler. "Come with Daddy, Jack."

When the door closed behind them, Olivia glanced at Luc who nodded and faced the teenager. "Tell me, Holly, is anything bothering you?"

The teenager's mutinous attitude reminded her of Melissa on a very bad day, but her daughter was by far more pleasant. Of course Melissa was surrounded with love and all the niceties money could buy. And she'd never faced an emotional crisis.

Oh God, how would Melissa react when Olivia talked to her about her father?

"I don't want to live at home," Holly said.

"Can you explain why?"

"I hate him." Her eyes widened with fury.

"Why?"

The girl turned toward her mother. "Because he's trying to act like he's my dad. 'Don't do this, Holly. Don't do that, Holly.' I don't want him around. He can't replace my father."

Olivia studied the mother's pained expression, but she knew better than to ask about the whereabouts of Holly's father.

"Her father left us when she was two and never came back," Teresa volunteered.

"And Jack's father left us before Jack was born, and this one will leave you too, Mom. You'll see. You don't know how to find a good man."

Olivia hated seeing the daughter attacking her mother with such bitterness.

Luc cleared his throat. "Holly, has Emilio ever been mean to you? I mean, abused or hit you."

She shrugged. "No, he wouldn't dare."

"Have you ever tried to be nice to him?" Luc continued his line of questioning.

"Why should I?"

"Holly, do you love your mother?"

The girl gasped. "Of course I love her, but she acts so stupid. I told her not to marry him. All we got is a new baby to feed and change all day long."

"And you don't like that?"

"No, I hate being poor. I hate wasting my time on a baby. I wanna live with my grandmother."

"If that's what you want, you can move tomorrow," Teresa said on a sigh.

The girl's gaze flew to her mother, sudden fear in her brown eyes. "What will you do without me? You can't take care of both babies. You'll be sick forever."

"I'm not going to force you to stay. I'll manage."

Holly frowned. "How? You always say you can manage and then you collapse. And I feel guilty. And I can't sleep at night when I hear you crying." Tears welled in her eyes.

Teresa touched her daughter's shoulder. "Somehow we'll work it out."

"No, Mom. I can't leave you. I'd never forgive myself if...if..." She lowered her head and sniffled.

"I want to see you happy, Holly. Then I may be able to take care of myself."

Holly shook her head. "You're too tired. And you have so much to do. I can't just abandon you and deal with the guilt." She bit her lip and glanced at Olivia, as if expecting help with her decision. "How about if I spend the weekend at grandma's? I'll stay home the rest of the week and help you after school."

"You'd do that, darling? Thank you." Teresa opened her arms to her daughter. "And will you try to be polite to Emilio? I want to keep him."

The girl mumbled, "I'll try."

Olivia sighed in relief. "Teresa, continue your medicine exactly as prescribed. You'll hear from a social worker soon. I want to see you in two weeks." She walked them to the registration area where Emilio waited with the small children.

"We found a solution," Teresa told her husband. "I'll tell you everything in the car."

Olivia let the adults gather their children and went back to the consultation room, eager for a moment of quiet to cool her aching nerves.

"This was a precedent. A whole family instead of one patient." Luc shook his head, his gaze fixed on her. "How are you feeling?"

"I badly need an aspirin. Teenagers are the most difficult patients to work with. It's tough to predict how they'll react." The day was far from over. Soon she'd have to deal with another teenager in a far more difficult confrontation.

She fumbled in her purse for a small bottle and extracted a coated capsule. As she swallowed it with a glass of water, a piercing female voice interrupted by male grumbling wafted through the door.

"What now? I hope the Tarinos are not fighting again," Olivia muttered, her headache escalating to a peak.

The door swung open admitting a tall blond man, followed by the receptionist.

****

Olivia gasped.

Him. Face to face after seventeen years.

His scowl melted, replaced by surprise as he stared at her.

Her hand flew to her heart to clutch her metallic

name tag. Her legs leaden, she stared at him and forgot to breathe.

"Dr. Luc, I tried to stop him, but he wouldn't listen," the receptionist said, her face red and her hand brandishing a pen as if she was debating whether to stab the intruder.

"Mr. Rutherford, what are you doing here?" Luc barked and stepped forward, hiding Olivia behind his tall frame.

I hope he didn't recognize me. Her jaws slack, she cringed behind Luc, her heart pounding against her ribs.

Jeremy tilted his head to the side. She glimpsed his curious grin. Luc followed suit, shifting in the same direction. "I have to talk to you, Dr. Lucien. When I called for an appointment, this woman said you were with patients."

"You should have waited for me to call you back." Luc's angry tone snapped her out of her panic.

Take a deep breath and count to ten. Still rooted to the floor, Olivia counted to twenty and then to thirty.

He can't hurt me. I am stronger. Her fingers clasping her name tag relaxed, and then tightened again.

Yes, but he can hurt Melissa. Another deep breath. The stiffness in her back ebbed, but her heartbeat was still running out of control.

This is ridiculous. You need to get out of here, her brain scolded.

"I don't have all day." Jeremy shrugged, completely at ease. "Instead of wasting my time waiting for you to call back, I decided to stop by. I waited outside. When I saw your patients leave, I came in. As simple as that. Do you still have a patient?" Frowning, he craned his neck to look behind Luc.

"No. Have a seat." Luc indicated a chair and

gestured to the receptionist to leave.

Was Luc planning to keep Jeremy here for an analysis session?

Olivia was done cowering. Time to function and get out of here. She touched Luc's back to push him out of her way. But Luc turned toward her, enfolded her in his arms and cradled her head against his shoulder.

"My love, I will walk you out." He swiftly slid to the door with her nestled against him.

Bless you, Luc.

Jeremy burst out laughing. "Ha ha. I caught you playing hanky-panky with a pretty nurse. Don't worry, Luc, I won't report you. I'm an understanding guy."

"Calm down and go," Luc whispered against her ear. "*Chérie*," he raised his voice, "I will pick you up in half an hour for dinner." He entered the consultation room and closed the door behind him.

Olivia took another deep breath and wet her lips. Jeremy's voice reached her. "You're head over heels for her, you son of a gun. She's a pretty morsel."

A moment of silence. She pictured the sarcastic smile accompanying Jeremy's condescending tone.

"Strange, she looks familiar. I wonder..."

Oh my God. Her bravado crumbled. She forced herself to navigate the reception area with a steady pace, but once in the corridor, she rushed to the Psychiatric Department and locked herself in her office.

****

"Amazing. There's this feeling of déjà vu," Jeremy mused as Luc observed him from under hooded eyes. Had Jeremy recognized the young student from his past? Luc had better distract him.

"How have you felt since our last session, Mr. Rutherford?" Luc shot out his routine question, while struggling not to tell his reluctant patient to get the hell out of here and let him check on Olivia.

"Cut the crap, Lucien. I'm not here to listen to your psychiatric jargon."

Keeping a tight leash on his temper, Luc narrowed his eyes and fixed Jeremy with a warning look. "I would appreciate you addressing me as Doctor and keeping a civil tongue." For a moment, their gazes dueled as fiercely as the sharp blades of swords. "And you can leave any time, sir."

Jeremy sneered but lowered his eyes. "You know you have me cornered, *Doc-tor*."

"Why is that? Has anything changed since last time?" Luc tented his fingers. In spite of his exasperation with Jeremy's insolence, his patient's last sentence intrigued him.

"The police came to interrogate me. I told the detective I was your patient. I insisted you wouldn't tolerate them harassing me and exacerbating my medical problems. Now, you better not contradict me."

"Mr. Rutherford, the police have nothing to do with any medical conditions you may have."

"You have to talk to them, Dr. Lucien. I came specifically to ask for your help." For a moment, Luc doubted his ears. Jeremy asking politely, almost begging? That was a precedent. "As my doctor, you have to protect me." The politeness melted. Jeremy was back into his arrogant skin. "I am paying exorbitant sums for your consultation. You'd better earn your fees."

Lips pinched, Luc gripped his wrist, so as not to throw a punch at the jerk goading him. "Mr. Rutherford, I will prescribe an anti-anxiety medicine to help you relax."

"I don't need your medicine. I want you to talk to these idiots at the police department."

Refusing to be intimidated, Luc scribbled in his

prescription notebook and handed the sheet to Jeremy. "Take one pill in the morning."

Jeremy glared at the prescription and huffed, but pocketed it. "Okay, I'll do as you say. But you owe me your help. Come with me to the police station."

Praying for patience, Luc stood. "Mr. Rutherford, psychiatrists don't go to the police to protect their patients. If we are subpoenaed as medical witnesses in a case, we testify on our patients' sanity, or insanity."

"You testify on your patient's...hmm." Jeremy scowled, considering Luc for a moment, but then he shrugged. "If it comes to that, we'll plead insanity. I count on your integrity to tell the court that I'm your patient and I'm innocent."

"I will tell the court my professional opinion on your medical problems," Luc said, keeping his voice under control.

"Good." Jeremy nodded. His scowl relaxed. "See you next week, at our scheduled appointment." He smiled, reverting to his charming side. "By the way, she's really cute. And hot. Have fun tonight." He stopped at the door and turned around. "If only I could remember why she seems so familiar. What's her name?" he asked curiously.

Luc arched an ominous brow. "My fiancée is off limits to my patients. Have a good evening, Mr. Rutherford."

"You fiancée?" Jeremy chuckled.

Luc glared, not liking one bit the interest gleaming in Jeremy's eyes. Jeremy had never had qualms about going after other men's fiancées or even wives.

****

Too restless to sit at her desk, Olivia had spent the last half hour pacing her office. Jeremy hadn't recognized her. The sophisticated image she presented now was a far cry from the skinny college girl with long chestnut hair. But the color of her eyes and her features hadn't changed and might trigger his memory. His last sentence about her looking familiar scared the bejesus out of her.

In spite of her shock, she'd instinctively hidden her badge so he wouldn't know her identity. With Jeremy's taste for women and his habit of going after anything that caught his fancy, would he try to discover who she was?

Once her initial fear subsided, she'd been ready to walk past him her chin high, and to hell with the consequences. Luc had stopped her with his little flirtatious game, and she'd played along because it was safer than confronting Jeremy—both for her and for Melissa.

Would he eventually remember her?

He might.

Whether he remembered her or ran into her again, she'd better be ready for any eventuality before exposing her innocent daughter to a traumatic encounter.

Olivia had told Luc she'd talk to Melissa although she hadn't been convinced it was the right thing to do. But now...

Now, Jeremy was here. At the Crisis Center. He'd been in Olivia's consultation room a few minutes ago and proved once more that nothing stopped him from imposing his will.

What if he bumped into her again? Or worse, into Melissa? What if he noticed his daughter's resemblance?

Olivia sagged onto her chair and licked a drop of blood at the corner of her lower lip. She hadn't noticed she'd been biting her lips that hard.

Would Jeremy hurt Melissa?

Or would he befriend his lovely daughter, now that she was grown up and not a burden? He might even shower her with gifts and try to turn her against her mother.

Melissa wanted a father so badly. She'd hate her mother for lying to her all these years. Olivia would lose her.

Oh God.

Olivia's head dropped as she wrestled with her conscience, her deepest beliefs and her fears. She dreaded upsetting her daughter's peace of mind, but there was no escape.

Jeremy was here.

Bile rose in Olivia's throat, and she doubled over.

Did she have any choice now?

Come on. Shake it off.

Raising her head, Olivia stared at the door. She shouldn't fear him. She'd fight him with all her strength.

Determination tightened her jaws.

She would confess everything to Melissa, explain the past, and assure her daughter that only she had mattered in her life. Hopefully Melissa would accept her explanations. She might still insist on meeting her father, but at least she'd be prepared, she'd know what sort of man he was.

The need to tell her daughter the truth cemented in her head.

A knock on the door jolted her out of her internal discussion. "Yes?"

"Olivia, it's me."

She unlocked and opened the door, sighing with relief as Luc walked in. He gathered her in his arms.

"I am sorry, *chérie*. I know it was a shock for you," he said, smoothing her hair with a gentle hand. She relaxed and leaned into him, absorbing his scent and strength with every pore of her body.

"Why was he here today?"

"A detective had interrogated him. In spite of his

bravado, Jeremy is scared. He said he counts on my protection in court. He wants me to testify on his behalf."

"Pathetic." She shook her head. "If I wasn't worried about Melissa, I'd laugh at his stupidity. That idiot doesn't know he has a psychiatrist who never lies."

"Let's not talk about him now. How do you feel?" He lifted her chin with his finger and captured her gaze.

"Better. I've been thinking a lot. Cincinnati is not a big city. I may run into him again. Imagine if Melissa is with me."

This was a subject Olivia needed to discuss with a cool head, and Lord knew she'd never remain composed in Luc's arms. Sighing, she stepped back. "You were right. I have to talk to her. The sooner the better."

"Good." He nodded and smiled, his eyes reflecting approval and respect. "In that case, we should go to your mother's house right away."

Olivia grabbed her purse and yanked her coat from the hook behind the door, not bothering to take her laptop. Tonight would be totally reserved for Melissa. Tonight would be the most stressful night of her life.

Melissa, my baby, I hope you'll understand and forgive.

Olivia's stomach knotted. Tonight...

Oh God, help us survive tonight.

Chapter Fifteen

Luc drove in silence for a while and then threw a look at Olivia. Eyes narrowed, she stared straight ahead, deep in her thoughts.

"How are you doing?"

"Okay, I guess."

"Are you having second thoughts?"

"I've made up my mind to talk to her. And I will."

He reached out and squeezed her hand. "I admire you for doing this. I know it's not easy." He glanced at her again. She was chewing on her lower lip. "Olivia, I am sorry if I have pushed you too hard. It's not only for your daughter. It's also for yourself, for your future." He tapped the steering wheel. "For us."

"Us?" She looked at him, with a sad lopsided smile.

"Once the way is clear, we will be able to plan a future for us."

She shook her head. "I've tried to dream of a future. Many times. But... Look what happened this afternoon. With every passing day, new obstacles arise."

"*Non, mon amour*. We will remove them one by one."

"Luc, I'll talk to Melissa, not only because she's entitled to know the truth, but also because I can't continue to live with this heavy burden. I can't continue to fear that she'll run into her father. I'm also doing it because...because I want to be free to come to you without seeing reproach in your eyes."

"I never realized—"

"You're very strict in your quest for truth. Somehow I always feel you're comparing me to that woman in your past who's responsible for your son's death. I don't want to fail in your eyes anymore."

"Oh, *mon amour*." He was tempted to stop the car, take her in his arms and prove to her how much he loved her. He'd been so worried about her when Jeremy had barged into the consultation room. Later when he'd noticed Jeremy's interest in Olivia, he'd struggled not to punch him. Luc had been jealous. He, the man who despised jealousy as an irrational feeling.

"I just hope I don't mess up with Melissa."

"Tell her everything, Olivia. Don't skip details about her brutal father to protect her. Once she knows the sordid truth, she will understand you and admire you." He extended his arm to stroke her hair in a soothing caress.

She snorted. "I wish I had your faith."

"Remember the girl we met this afternoon. My first impression was that she hated her mother."

"Me too. I couldn't believe it when she refused to leave home and insisted she had to stay and help her mother."

"See? And Melissa is by far a nicer girl. She loves you. She may be shocked at first, but once she adjusts to the news, she will appreciate all you did for her." They were about to reach her mother's house. "Olivia, do you want to talk to her before or after dinner?"

"After."

He smiled. "Good. Marianna has promised a duck *à l'orange*. You will be in a better shape after eating."

"I can't believe it. You act like a kid deprived of food."

"In a way, I am. I don't cook, so I survive on

restaurant meals and fast food. Your mother's cooking is incredible." He turned into the driveway and cut the engine. "Ready?"

"Yes." She gathered her purse and jacket. "Let's go."

Amazing Olivia. She was running on sheer willpower. She'd already shoved her feelings aside to deal with the problem at hand. Luc climbed out of the car and went around to open the door for her. She straightened and squared her shoulders. As she put one foot out, he bent and pressed his lips to the back of her hand and then he turned it and kissed her palm.

He raised his head. A streak of pain danced in her bluish-green eyes, the only sign of emotion in her otherwise calm attitude. It sucker-punched him straight in the gut.

Had he been wrong to put so much pressure on her? Was the specter of his own past haunting him to the point of skewing his judgment? Should he have kept his mouth shut?

****

Olivia entered her mother's house as if she were crossing the board exam room. Except that tonight her heart reeled in a pathetic, busted shape and ruled over her usually sharp mind. The rest of her life and her daughter's peace of mind depended on tonight's events, on Olivia's ability to convince Melissa of her genuine motivation to protect her, on Melissa's reaction to her mother's revelations.

Clutching Luc's hand, Olivia paused for a minute in the living room and surveyed it as if seeing it for the last time. She wanted to memorize every happy moment she'd ever spent here with Melissa.

"*Chérie*, don't torture yourself," Luc murmured against her hair as he wrapped his arms around her waist.

"Hello." Marianna welcomed them with a smile that stretched to her ears. "Oh, sorry. I still have a lot to do in the kitchen," she called over her shoulder as she scurried away.

"Mom, please, come back here." Olivia wiggled out of Luc's arms and sighed. "I can't believe it. She's going to sit in the kitchen for an hour to give us privacy." With Luc following in her steps, she strode to her mother's haven. "Mom, where's Melissa?"

"She'll be here any minute. She went to see Christine, the girl who's going to France with her. But—" Mama narrowed her eyes, scanning and assessing Olivia's face. "What's wrong with you, *bambina*? You look sick." She reached out and touched her forehead.

"No, Mom. I'm not sick. Just apprehensive. I've decided to talk to Melissa tonight."

"To talk...you mean about her... Oh God." Mama touched her left breast, rubbing her heart. "Tonight?"

"Isn't that what you've wanted me to do for a long time?"

"Yeah, yeah, just wait until after dinner. I made the duck *à l'orange*. I don't want it to go to waste if...if things don't work well."

"I can't believe what I'm hearing. Thanks for the encouragement. Honestly, Mom."

"I'm sorry, *bambina*. You just took me by surprise." Mama reached for the bowl of chocolates, popped one in her mouth and handed another to Olivia. "Take one. It'll help you calm down."

"Give me another while you're at it. Luc, a chocolate?"

"No, thanks. I'll wait for the duck and the cannelloni. By the way, Marianna, what's that delicious smell coming from your kitchen?" He sniffed and sighed dramatically as he rubbed his stomach. "Garlic and orange and—?"

"Ah, my recipe is a secret. I will only tell you I added a liqueur, Grand Marnier, and some sherry."

Luc inhaled with a flourish. "Divine."

Olivia shook her head and snorted. "French flattery by an expert."

"I'm home. Hi Mom, Luc," Melissa called as she banged the front door behind her and came to hug Olivia. When Melissa turned and kissed Luc three times on his cheeks, Olivia's heart fell to her toes. Her daughter already behaved like a French teenager greeting a loving *papa*.

"Well let's eat right away since you're back, sweetheart," Mama said, with a meaningful nod to Olivia. "Come to the kitchen and help. Here, Luc, you take the duck platter and, Olivia, take the cannelloni. I'll bring the salad. Melissa, don't forget the garlic bread."

When they all settled around the table, Mama said grace, but her voice broke when she asked the Lord to give wisdom and happiness to everyone.

Please, let things work out well.

Olivia murmured amen and met Luc's intense gaze.

While Mama served everyone, Luc poured the wine for the adults and a Coke for Melissa.

"I had a fantastic afternoon," Melissa chimed.

Olivia hardly heard the stories her daughter related or Luc's questions and comments. She sliced her meat into small pieces and then smaller ones. The first bite she swallowed lodged in her throat. It took a whole glass of wine to force it down.

For a change, Mama was silent and didn't urge Olivia to eat, but her intermittent sighs grew louder by the minute. As soon as Luc cleared his plate, she ordered, "Olivia dear, can you bring the tiramisu from the fridge?"

"Nana, it was really delicious."

Melissa and Luc had honored the dinner with a

healthy appetite, but Marianna hardly smiled.

Either Mama's theory about the soothing effect of chocolate had failed for once, or maybe she hadn't loaded her cake with enough chocolate. By the time Melissa finished her dessert, Olivia was a wretched mass of nerves.

"Can we adjourn to the living room?" Luc asked, his question sounding the gong. Her heart beating erratically, Olivia lurched forward. Their gazes collided, and he gently smiled.

"Yes, let's sit and talk for a moment." That was it. No backing out now. She walked to the living room and dropped into an armchair, quickly rehearsing her opening sentences.

"Good," Melissa said. "Luc, we can talk some more about my trip."

Marianna retreated to the kitchen. Luc filled two after-dinner drinks and handed one to Olivia. She sipped the burning liquor, set her glass on the cocktail table and laced her fingers in her lap.

Olivia threw a look at Luc and then turned to face her daughter. "Melissa, there's something I want to tell you."

Melissa glanced at Luc and then at her mother, and giggled. "Gee, I bet I know what it is, Mom. No wonder you're so nervous. Don't worry, you have my blessing."

"What?" Olivia frowned at the joyful and ironical expression on her daughter's face. Oh dear, Melissa thought that she and Luc were going to announce—

"No, that's not what I want to say." Olivia lost the track of her thoughts.

"Really, Mom?" Her daughter laughed, mouth puckered in disbelief. "Come on."

"No, Melissa, no. I have to tell you about your birth." God, that's not what she was supposed to say. She closed her eyes trying to remember her speech. Only jumbled words came to her lips. "Your natural father... I mean I got pregnant when I was eighteen. We weren't married and he didn't...he couldn't...I mean I couldn't..."

"Couldn't what, Mom?" Melissa nudged with a smile while visibly at a loss on making sense of her mother's words.

"I wanted you very much, darling. But..." Olivia slapped her fingers across her lips.

God, it wasn't coming out the right way at all. Guilt flooded her.

"But what, Mom? You wanted to have an abortion, because you were eighteen and not married?" The laughter had disappeared from her daughter's voice, replaced by a cold, metallic hiss.

The room seemed to rotate around Olivia. She gripped the arms of her chair. "No, no, that's not right. *He* didn't want a child. I had to leave him. Your grandparents helped me raise you."

Wrong words. What was she supposed to say?

Her mind blanked. Her breath escaped her lungs, rushing out over her lips.

"You left him when he had to go to war? How could you?" Melissa's eyes filled with anger and disbelief.

"He never went to war. He never saved anybody."

Melissa gasped and raised both hands, palm up. "What are you trying to tell me? He didn't die at war?"

"No, no." Olivia gulped, seizing the twist she hadn't anticipated and trying to come up with answers that wouldn't sound damning. Where was her speech and the motherly words she'd prepared to soothe Melissa?

"Then how did he die?" Melissa leaned forward, squinting like a prosecution lawyer.

Olivia lowered her lashes, her throat tightened by the implacable rope of her memories. "He didn't die, but listen—"

Melissa bolted out of the sofa. "My father didn't die? He's alive. Alive," she screamed in a hysterical fit. "You let me believe he died? You deprived me of my dad for my whole life? How could you, Mom?" She strode to Olivia's chair and bent toward her, smacking her hands on both arms of the chair. "How could you lie to me all that time?" She groaned, her face a few inches from Olivia's.

Luc came beside Olivia's chair and touched her shoulder. "Olivia, tell her the whole truth about him." She heard Luc's voice through a haze.

"There are more lies?" Melissa snarled, her glare flicking from Olivia to Luc.

Lord, how did her explanation degenerate into such a damning imbroglio? "Darling, calm down. Let me explain."

"I don't want to hear more of your lies. I hate you." The look Melissa gave her broke her heart. Her baby was suffering. Because of her.

"Tell her what kind of a man he was," Luc urged, squeezing her shoulder.

But she couldn't. She'd done enough damage for one night. Her daughter shook with anger, obviously determined to disregard any justification coming from Olivia.

"I don't want to see you again." Melissa spat the words as she straightened and backed up from Olivia's chair, her lips pursed into a thin line "I want to find my father. I have to meet him." She sobbed and hiccupped. "I have a father. A real father." She marched toward the hallway.

Olivia staggered behind her, arms stretched in supplication. "Darling, wait, please."

"Melissa, give your mother the chance to tell you the whole story as it happened," Luc said in the soothing voice he used with his patients.

How on earth could he remain calm at a moment

like this?

Melissa stopped, made a complete volte-face, and her features hardened. “You, stay out of it. You’re no better than her.” She turned to Olivia. “What’s my dad’s real name? I assume Joe Madden is a lie too. Who’s my father?”

Olivia shook her head. If she told Melissa her father’s name, now, her daughter might run away to him and she’d lose her forever.

“I’ll find out,” Melissa screamed, big tears rolling down her cheeks, as she ran toward her room. “And when I find out, I’ll go to him, and you’ll never see me again, you liar.”

Chapter Sixteen

"Melissa, my darling, please come back." Olivia's cry broke Luc's heart.

"Olivia," he said, coming toward her.

She ignored him and remained frozen in the middle of the living room, arms outstretched and chin tipped toward the second floor landing where Melissa had disappeared. A moment later a door banged.

Olivia lowered her head and dropped her arms to her sides. Staring at the Oriental rug, she remained rooted in place. "I've lost her. I've lost my daughter."

"*Chérie*, why didn't you tell her the whole story? Why didn't you explain that Jeremy threw you out and didn't want her?"

She slowly raised her head, a heartrending expression on her face. "I couldn't. Everything went too fast. The wrong way. She was too shocked, too disappointed. I couldn't add to it."

Luc stepped forward and took her hands in his, trying to impart his strength to her. "There is still time to fix the damage. Go to her room. Tell her about his abusive streak."

"No, Luc." Olivia snatched her hands from his and clutched the front of her shirt. "I have to give her space," she said, her voice controlled.

Though she was wounded and hurting with a pain sharper than a physical blow, she'd calmed down. "Melissa needs time to assimilate what she's just heard."

He'd never seen so much suffering on a woman's

face. His beautiful Olivia seemed to have aged in a matter of minutes. Because of his advice to reveal the truth. A strange way to practice his Hippocratic Oath. *Do no harm.* He'd just harmed both the woman he loved and her daughter.

"I'm sorry, Olivia. I shouldn't have interfered. You were right. I was arrogant in my inflexible search for the truth." And yet, he would continue to advocate his principles. He'd never change his mind about the need to reveal the truth.

"I'm not blaming you, Luc." Her gaze rose to meet his. Tears and desolation shimmered in her aqua eyes. "I took the wrong approach from the beginning. I walked into quicksand and kept going. With every passing day, I dug my own grave deeper and deeper."

She slumped onto the sofa, leaned against the back as if she'd been drained of every ounce of energy, and closed her eyes. Luc filled two glasses of Cognac. "Have a drink. It will help."

Without opening her eyes, she shook her head. He swirled the liquor in his glass, inhaled the alcohol's sweet fragrance and chugged it down.

He put the glass on the cocktail table and sat beside her.

"I pushed you to talk to her."

"But it was my decision to do it."

He could feel her pain, the headache hammering the side of her face all the way to her skull. With gentle strokes, he rubbed her temples and forehead and raked his fingers through her hair.

"Let her cool off tonight, and tomorrow tell her about her father's character."

"She's already decided I'm the worst mother on earth. She won't believe a word I say."

"Would you allow me to talk to her?" He cupped her face between his hands. "I can be convincing in explaining what a wonderful woman you are."

"Thank you, Luc." She looked at him, sadness and regret shadowing her beautiful eyes. "I blew it all, years ago. Unfortunately, it's too late now."

"What are you talking about? Nothing is too late." He'd never seen her like this. Anxious and perturbed, even defeated. He wrapped his arms around her back and pulled her against him. "*Chérie*, you're a strong woman, a good psychiatrist. It's only a crisis, and we will solve it together." He smiled at her and caressed her cheek. "Olivia, I am here for you."

"You don't know much about adolescents." She snorted, a hysterical noise that saddened him more than cries. "Besides, there's no *together* anymore."

"Excuse me?" He pulled back in shock. "Do you realize what you are saying?"

"Please, Luc, don't insist."

"I can't let you face this alone. Are you pushing me away?"

"Can't you understand? I don't want this," she said, her voice rising. "But with you around, I'll be distracted, unable to concentrate on Melissa. I have to take care of my daughter. On my own."

"You have to?" He scowled and gripped her shoulders. "Olivia, please, enough with your false sense of duty."

She shook her head, a frown of despair marring her forehead. "Please, Luc, leave." He hardly heard the inaudible murmur.

"Pardon?" Her words torpedoed his feelings and dreams. He scooted away.

"Give me space." She looked at him, silent appeal in her eyes. "I messed up again and I need to fix this mess before it's too late." She was back in control, her face devoid of expression.

His stomach clenched at the magnitude of her request. *To go back to their earlier strained relationship.* Like two strangers, with him tiptoeing around her feelings, after she had claimed only a few hours ago she loved him.

Unable to sit still, he paced the living room, filled his glass and drained it, paused and turned toward her, his fingers fisted against his sides. "You will destroy our hopes of happiness because of Melissa? Again?"

"I don't expect you to understand a mother's feelings." Her gaze flicked toward the hallway where her daughter had flown. "Melissa is all I have. I don't want to be sidetracked by your presence and lose her."

His blood boiling, Luc contemplated Olivia as if he'd never seen her before. How could he have been so wrong about her? He'd been treading carefully this time. Yet he'd made the same mistake. Twice.

She claimed she cared about him. Obviously not enough. Not the way he wanted her to love him.

"Do you want me to leave forever?" he asked, his scowl deepening.

"Yes." She kept her eyes fixed on the hallway.

If he left this house, it would be forever. He'd suffer a hundred deaths, but he'd erase her from his heart eventually. He wanted to walk away, but couldn't get himself to move one inch. *Get out. Go.* But first...

"Are you sure, Olivia?"

"Yes."

But he couldn't let her handle the crisis alone. "Look me in the eyes then, and tell me you don't love me."

She lowered her head.

"Tell me our lovemaking was a sham. Lust with no feelings."

Her fingers trembled. She laced them together and buried them in her lap.

"Well, tell me."

"I can't. Last night was the most beautiful night

of my life." She raised her head.

Love blurred with fear in the aqua eyes he treasured.

"Thank you," he said, exhaling with relief.

She blinked and averted her gaze. "But I need to be alone with Melissa from now on to make up for hurting her so much."

"You can't think rationally now. I will leave you. But I will be back tomorrow." He strode to the hall and turned around. "Olivia, just remember I love you. And I love Melissa as if she were my own."

She groaned as he yanked his raincoat from the guest closet and opened the front door.

Outside, the weather matched his stormy mood. As he stomped out in the night, lightning ripped through the sky. A mix of hail and icy rain pelted his face and slithered down his neck. He ran to his car. Cursing the long drive ahead of him in the foul weather, he turned on the ignition. In spite of the windshield wipers flicking at top speed, he could hardly see a thing.

As he started backing out of the driveway, floodlights illuminated the area. The garage door opened. Marianna ran out, and Olivia slid into her van. Luc slammed on the brakes, climbed out of the car and sprinted to the garage while thunder clapped in the distance.

"What's wrong?"

He strained to hear Marianna's shout. "Melissa's missing. She took my old Cadillac. Olivia is going to look for her."

"Olivia, come with me. I will drive. You call her friends."

Olivia didn't hesitate or argue when Luc ordered her out of her van. Her mother handed Luc an umbrella. He held it above her while they ran to his car.

As soon as she sat in the passenger seat, she

pulled out her cell phone. “Luc, turn left, then go straight.” She pushed a speed dial button. “Stephanie, did you talk to Melissa in the last hour?” On the negative answer, she tried a few more numbers.

“There is a *Y* in the road, shall I go left or right?”

“Try right. I’m calling her friend Christine who lives off this road.” Olivia punched another number. “Christine, is Melissa at your place?” She didn’t like the girl’s hesitation. “I’m worried about her. Is she with you?”

“I’m sorry, Dr. Crane. She was here before dinner. Later on, she called me from her cell phone. She was crying and said she was on her way to Jennifer’s.”

“Thank you.” Olivia tried another number. “Jennifer, this is Dr. Crane. Is Melissa here?”

“No. Dr. Crane, she...she said she was coming. But...she hasn’t arrived yet.” Olivia shivered at the girl’s stuttering.

“When did she call you?”

“A half hour ago.”

“Oh God.” Olivia snapped the phone shut. “Luc, make a U-turn. Go back to the *Y* and take a left. Melissa should have been at Jennifer’s house long ago. Oh my God.” Olivia’s stomach somersaulted. Was her baby lost and hurt, alone in the bleak night?

Luc swerved and reversed direction. At the intersection, he turned left, decreased his speed and switched on the high beam. The headlights sliced through the shimmering curtain of icy rain, and the car crawled under a gloomy arch of naked branches. Olivia flicked her gaze right and left, trying to pierce the blackness of the night beyond the beam of light.

Please, please let Melissa be safe.

“On the right.”

Luc’s voice prickled her heart as he seized her

hand and squeezed it.

Her head swiveled to the right. She saw the car.

The Cadillac hunkered on the side, hood pitched into the ditch, its left bumper smashed against the trunk of a tree.

"Melissa." The scream shot out of Olivia's lungs. "Luc, stop." But he'd already slowed to a crawl and turned off the engine.

Olivia leaped out of the car and ran to the Cadillac, slipping and sliding on the icy surface. Luc pulled her up against him and held her elbow, forcing her to a steady pace until they reached the driver's side. She peered in through the glass. Melissa was slouched against the window.

Luc jerked the door handle and pulled with all his strength. "It's stuck."

"Luc, do something, please." She pummeled on the glass, her eyes fixed on her daughter's head.

"Call 911. I'll go in from the other door," he said, as he circled the car.

She punched the number and asked for help, while following Luc to the other side of the car. He picked up a stone and smashed the window on the passenger side. Taking off his raincoat, he wrapped a sleeve around his fist, reached inside and slipped the lock up. He opened the door, swiped the broken glass away and slid inside the car.

Olivia bent over him to look at Melissa. "Oh my God."

"Melissa?" Luc called. "She's unconscious."

Olivia thought her own heart was about to stop.

Luc took Melissa's hand and felt for a pulse. "She's alive, but she's squashed between the door and the airbag. Move out of the way, Olivia."

Tears streamed down Olivia's cheeks as Luc unsnapped the seatbelt and edged her daughter away from the airbag to the passenger seat. "Leave her in the car. It's too wet outside. The ambulance will be here any minute."

"Sit beside her. You are soaked. I wish I had a stethoscope."

"A stethoscope? Doc always keeps an emergency medical kit and a flashlight in his trunk."

Luc left for a minute and returned with the items. Olivia wrapped the pressure cuff around Melissa's arm, plugged the stethoscope in her ears and listened. "90 over 50. Her BP is way too low."

"To be expected when she's in shock." He moved the flashlight over Melissa's face and paused, illuminating the left side of her head. "The air bag protected her from the worst of the impact, but her head must have hit the side window."

Olivia followed the beam of light, touched a spot on her daughter's left temple and froze. She rubbed her fingers together. "Luc, she's bleeding. Oh God."

A siren pierced the silence of the road. Police cars and EMS squads surrounded them. Olivia got out of the car.

"I am Dr. Luc from CUH and this is Dr. Crane, the girl's mother." In a few words he explained the situation to one of the paramedics while the other two laid Melissa on a wooden board and immobilized her cervical spine with a neck brace. After moving her onto a stretcher, they rolled her into the ambulance.

"You better go with them, Olivia. I will follow and see you at the hospital." He turned to one of the paramedics. "Can Dr. Crane ride with her daughter?"

"Go ahead, Dr. Crane," the man said as he held the door open for her.

The familiar antiseptic smells soothed her. She sat in the ambulance watching while the paramedics measured Melissa's vitals. "Is her blood pressure still low?"

"Yes." A paramedic put an oxygen mask over

Melissa's nose, swabbed the bruise on her temple and applied a pressure dressing. Another set up an IV drip and then placed patches on her chest for an electrocardiogram.

Melissa's irregular breathing twittered out of her open lips while her chest rose and slumped.

"Darling, can you hear me? It's Mom."

Melissa's eyelashes fluttered and she stirred, inhaling deeply.

"Darling?"

"She's coming around," the paramedic said.

Now that they were on their way to the hospital, Olivia's erratic pulse resumed a normal speed.

"Mom...scared...eyes." Melissa's voice was barely audible.

Eyes? What did she mean? Were her eyes hurting?

"I'm here, sweetheart. Don't be scared. Everything will be fine."

Melissa's fingers twitched as if she were trying to raise her hand, then her eyes widened in panic. "Mom. Can't move."

Olivia covered her daughter's hand with a warm embrace. "I know, sweetheart. We're in the ambulance. They've restrained you until a doctor can check you."

"Don't leave me, Mom."

Tears pooled in Olivia's eyes as she heard the wobbly voice.

"Never, baby. I promise. You'll be fine. I love you, darling. You're all I have."

Anxiety and regret twisted Olivia's guts. She'd caused the accident. By hiding the truth for years, choosing the wrong words to inform Melissa and then wallowing in self-pity, she'd almost killed her daughter.

How could she ever forgive herself? How could she make up for her lack of judgment?

When Melissa recovered, she'd tell her everything. Every detail. Would that be enough to repair the damage?

What if Melissa wanted to meet her father?

Olivia studied her daughter's features.

I'll go with you, my darling. I'll face him again, if that's what you want.

Chapter Seventeen

The trip to the hospital lasted an eternity. Finally, the ambulance stopped at the emergency entrance. Olivia walked beside the stretcher as the paramedics wheeled Melissa to a cubicle. The medical staff cut through Melissa's sodden clothes and removed them, and then dressed her in a blue and white striped gown and proceeded with a series of tests.

"Mom, it hurts." Melissa fingered her temple and head.

Her complaint broke Olivia's heart. "You'll get better soon." Olivia tried to project a conviction she was far from feeling.

The ER attending physician examined Melissa. As he touched her stomach, her scream of pain hit Olivia like a punch in the face. She knew something was wrong before the doctor said, "I'll order CAT scans on the head and body."

"How about her eyes?"

"No problem there."

Luc arrived soon after Melissa's gurney had been wheeled out of ER. "How is she feeling?"

"Her head hurts."

"A concussion?"

"Probably. And her stomach area is sore. I hope there's no internal bleeding." Olivia linked her hands and twisted her fingers.

"No need to panic. We'll know after the CAT scans."

Olivia turned to look at Luc. "Thank you." He'd been at her side every minute like a loving husband, even after she'd pushed him away.

"Do not even mention it."

"I'll never forgive myself if she has serious injuries."

"She is young and healthy. She will recover soon. And everything will go back to normal."

"What is normal in this case?"

"I don't know, Olivia. It can be whatever you decide to make it. Don't rush into any decisions now." He scanned her soaked clothes and wet hair, then opened a cabinet and rummaged through plastic wraps containing scrubs. He pulled out two packets and handed her one. "We better change or we will catch pneumonia."

He closed the privacy curtain and stepped out. She followed his advice, changed and dried her hair with a towel. When he came back garbed in scrubs, he appraised her with a smile. Faint amusement crinkled the corners of his eyes. "Cute. I have not seen you in one of these since your med school days."

She looked down at herself and then stared at him. "Oh."

Her mind leapt to the day she'd first met him, the French resident coming for a fellowship in the U.S. She winced at the reminder of a time she'd spent years trying to forget. What a waste.

Was it too late to make up? Too late to be happy? She had to dedicate every hour of her time to Melissa from now on. Would Luc stay and help them? After she'd pushed him away again?

He glanced at his watch. "Call Marianna. She must be out of her mind with worry by now."

"You're right." Her pulse still pinging through her veins, she nodded. Amazing Luc. Even in the middle of chaos, he thought about everyone. She dialed her home number and reassured her mother.

"Dr. Crane?" The ER attending physician stood at the cubicle entrance.

"Yes? How's Melissa?"

"She has a light concussion. Nothing too serious. We'll monitor her. It will heal with time." Olivia exhaled with relief. "But the CAT scan showed internal bleeding. We need to operate immediately on the spleen. I've already called the surgeon."

The blood drained from Olivia's face, and air clogged in her throat. She fisted her hands and forced herself to calm down. "Doctor, may I be present during the operation?"

The attending physician shook his head. "No way. You're her mother." He was right. But she'd promised Melissa she'd be with her. All the time.

Luc touched her arm. "Olivia, I will attend the surgery. And I will tell you every detail."

"Thank you, Luc."

"Nope," the ER doctor interfered. "This is not a teaching hospital. Other than the surgical staff assigned, no one else is allowed to be present. You'll be informed as soon as the surgery is finished."

"Can I at least see her now?" Her self-control in shreds, Olivia crossed her arms around herself, fighting tears.

"I'm sorry, Dr. Crane. They've already taken her to the OR," the ER physician said as he left the cubicle.

"It's my fault." She slumped against the wall and sobbed, headless of Luc and the nurses passing by outside the curtain. "If she has any permanent damage, I'll have caused it." Her child was suffering. But there was nothing a loving mother could do at the moment, except hope and pray.

Luc dragged around the privacy curtain and pulled her against his chest. "Hopefully, there will be no permanent damage. You have to believe it." His heart bled for the woman he loved and her daughter. He brushed away the hair mussing Olivia's face and wiped her tears with his fingers.

"*Chérie*, you are not helping her by torturing yourself."

She sniffled against his shoulder. He handed her a tissue.

"We cannot stay here any longer. Let's go to the waiting room." A hand on her back, he led her out of the ER cubicle toward the surgery department. He wanted to give her time to collect herself, move around, walk, do something. Anything was better than this collapse. "I think we can use some coffee."

She'd stopped crying, but she walked past the vending machine like a robot that had been set to perform only one task at a time.

The waiting room was deserted at that hour of the night. She drooped on the sofa and stared straight ahead. He shook his head, unsure how to treat her depression. Maybe because he was too emotionally close to her, too involved in her problems. His lips twitched into a grimace. He left her and raced to the vending machine, bought two cups of coffee and came back in record time. She was still in the same position, her gaze fixed on the wall.

He set the Styrofoam cups on the wooden cocktail table and sat on the sofa next to her. Hit by an image of his past, he frowned and studied her.

Like him years ago, Olivia had been clobbered with a real blow. The pain he'd experienced when he met his little son in a hospital bed clubbed him again, a recurrent nightmare he'd erased only by his unrelenting advocacy of the truth. He heard his own words strangled by emotion, "I am your Papa." The adorable toddler, a small, pale copy of his father, had looked blankly at him and closed his eyes. And never spoke to him.

"I understand your pain, Olivia. Not as a psychiatrist but as a father. You daughter is alive. Be grateful she is alive. And she is going to make it. My son died two hours after I met him."

Olivia finally turned toward him and acknowledged his presence. "I'm sorry, Luc." She bit her lip, anxiety wrinkling her beautiful face. "When we were in the ambulance, she asked me not to leave her. She still wants me after what I told her."

"Of course, she wants you. You are the mother she has always loved and will continue to love."

"I have to make up for my mistakes. If she wants to see her father, I will take her to him."

Luc rubbed his chin, not sure it was a good idea. He'd met Jeremy Rutherford twice and resented the bastard's lack of remorse for his violent and sexual misconduct. Luc suddenly realized that all his campaign for the truth could not justify exposing the love of his life to her horrific first boyfriend. "Why would you do that?"

"But Luc, you've been telling me for the past two months that I had to tell Melissa the truth. Are you having second thoughts now?"

"No, of course not."

"Well, she wants to meet her father."

Luc scowled, his heart pinched with a fierce protectiveness toward Olivia. Maybe the same protectiveness she felt toward Melissa. No, he said to himself. Not the same one. "No," he repeated in a loud voice. "There must be a better solution."

"Really? I'd like to hear it."

He relaxed. In a way, discussing Jeremy had taken Olivia's mind away from her anxiety about the crash and her daughter's surgery. At least for the moment. Keep her talking and arguing. "What if Jeremy does not want to see her?"

"That would be great. At least, we'd get rid of him once and for all."

"Yes, but Melissa will be devastated."

"For heaven's sake, Luc, stop being so negative. I'm trying to do the best I can for my daughter, within your sacrosanct boundaries of the truth."

He couldn't help smiling at the color that reddened Olivia's cheek. She was back to her old self. Strong and assertive. And scowling at him.

"What are you smiling at?"

"You look cute when you are upset."

"Bug off, Luc. I'm really not in a mood for flirting now." She flipped a wayward strand of hair away from her forehead.

He flexed his fingers, thinking hard and fast. Melissa wanted to know her father, and Olivia was ready to let her meet Jeremy. But Luc couldn't stand the idea of Olivia, or even Melissa, going to see the abusive *salaud,* especially after he'd seen interest for Olivia in Jeremy's eyes. Even though Jeremy was under house arrest in the Rutherford's mansion, God only knew what could happen during the encounter. Suddenly, Luc hit his forehead. *The grandfather*.

"I have an idea."

"What now?" Olivia threw him a dubious look.

"The grandfather."

"What about him?"

"I think Melissa would be happy to know him. He is family to her. A nice great-grandfather instead of a rotten father who didn't want her. Suppose you call Tom Rutherford and ask him to come and meet Melissa. He liked her a lot when he saw her. He's authoritative but courteous. He seemed to be a decent man. Nothing like Jeremy. Besides, he doesn't approve of his grandson's behavior."

"You think he would come all the way here?"

"Maybe we can go and see him. Or meet at the Crisis Center."

"I'll go to his house. I feel I have to do that."

"I will come with you."

"No, this is a family matter. I'll go alone."

He sprang from the sofa. Her high-handed way of shoving him aside wounded him to the core.

"You may not consider me part of your family,

Dr. Crane. But you have been part of my life for ten years." She jerked back, but her widened eyes didn't intimidate him. "Your own daughter had asked me to be her father at her dance. Your own daughter trusts me more than you do."

Her lips parted on a gasp as she tilted her head up. "Luc, I do. I swear I trust you more than anyone, but I have to—"

"You can't go alone to the Rutherford mansion. Period." He exhaled, exasperated by her twisted sense of motherly duty. "What if Jeremy is there? Are you ready to face him alone?"

"I'm not afraid of him anymore, now that Melissa knows the truth."

She squeezed her hands into fists. Luc smiled, not doubting for a second that she'd throw a punch in Jeremy's face if she had to. "But I'm not ready to let him see you again." Olivia was the woman he loved, and he owed her his protection, whether she wanted it or not.

"Dr. Crane?" A man in green scrubs entered the waiting room.

Olivia bolted from her seat at the same time Luc spun around.

"Yes?" she asked in a whisper.

"I'm Dr. Sloan. The surgery went well. We glued the spleen to stop the bleeding. Your daughter is in recovery."

Olivia's sigh of relief echoed Luc's. "Thank you, doctor. When can I see her?"

"In an hour. I don't expect complications. In a week we'll start therapy."

"Thank you." She nodded, and he left as a police officer entered the room, a paper bag in his hand.

"Mrs. Crane? Ma'am, I'm Officer Santino. May I ask you some questions about the accident?" The policeman didn't wait for an invitation to drop in a chair.

Olivia remained standing, visibly taken aback by the man's curt tone. Luc waved to the sofa. "We have a few minutes before Dr. Crane visits her daughter in recovery."

"Are you a rela—"

"A friend of the family, Dr. Vicourt-Michelet," Luc said, returning the man's cold stare.

"Mrs. Crane, we found this purse in the car. Is it your daughter's?" The policeman handed her the brown leather pouch.

"Yes."

"How old is the girl?"

"Sixteen."

"Good. She's over driving age. Although if she were my daughter I wouldn't have allowed her to drive at night in such a foul weather."

Olivia pursed her lips without answering.

"Can I see her driver's license, ma'am?"

Olivia threw an apprehensive gaze at Luc. He swallowed, hoping Melissa hadn't forgotten to take her permit with her. As Olivia fumbled in the purse, a forlorn grimace replaced her previous angst. "She must have left it at home."

"I see."

"We can send it to you as soon as we go home," Luc said, hating the police officer for adding to Olivia's troubles.

"Please do that. I'll have to suspend her anyway for driving without having a license with her."

At the moment, it was the least of their worries. Olivia shrugged.

"Of course, the smash wasn't your daughter's fault," the man added as if he regretted his previous rudeness.

"What do you mean? Do you know what caused the accident?" Luc asked, seizing the opportunity to divert the conversation.

"A deer. He must have run in front of her. Your

daughter probably swerved the car to avoid it, hit a tree and ended in a ditch."

Olivia's hand flew to her mouth. "Oh my God. The first thing she said in the ambulance was 'eyes'. That's what scared her in the dark."

"A deer?" Luc's breath caught in his throat. Melissa was lucky to have escaped with her life. Deer accidents could cause very serious injuries.

"My men found the dying deer not too far from the vehicle. Ma'am, I'll send you my report and the fine for driving without a license. If I were you, I'd keep a closer eye on my teenagers." He stood and left.

"What a lout," Luc muttered as the man disappeared in the corridor.

"Poor Melissa. It's not even her fault. It's all mine." Olivia pulled out her cell phone, a resolute expression on her face. "I'm calling information." She waited a few seconds. "May I have the number for Mr. Thomas Rutherford?"

Olivia scribbled the number on a piece of paper Luc handed her. Clasping her cell phone in her hand, she glanced at him, hesitating. "Maybe it would be better to wait until Melissa completely recovers from her surgery before asking Rutherford to meet her."

"Definitely, wait a day or two. I have the feeling that the accident may have temporarily erased some of her short term memory."

"Even if she's forgotten our conversation, I want her to meet her great-grandfather."

"Of course."

Luc sucked in a deep breath and gritted his teeth. No, it wasn't Melissa's fault. And it wasn't Olivia's either. He was the one responsible for starting this mess with his lack of understanding and his inflexibility. His throat constricted.

A deer accident. Olivia's daughter could have

died. Because of him.

When would he stop making a parallel between his experience with Brigitte and Olivia's painful past? He'd thought and acted like a shrink. And maybe like a resentful father.

He couldn't continue to interfere in Olivia's life as if he had all the answers. But he loved her and couldn't turn his back now just because guilt nagged his conscience. Definitely not now when both Olivia and Melissa needed him.

He would give Olivia the emotional space she'd asked for and act the perfect friend rather than the eager lover. Meanwhile he'd spend more time with Melissa, who could use a decent paternal figure after losing her childhood illusions about an honorable father and a normal family.

Oh, yes, he'd stick around in spite of Olivia's efforts to push him away. He was convinced that Olivia loved him and would come to him as soon as she regained full control of her emotions and Melissa's health improved.

Be patient, Lucien. He mumbled the mantra he'd been repeating to himself since he arrived in Cincinnati. *Patient.*

Chapter Eighteen

"Are we ready?" Melissa was going home after two painful weeks in a hospital room.

Two weeks during which Olivia's heart had thumped at an uneven rate, skipped a beat each time Melissa woke up screaming from a nightmare, slowed when Melissa cried from pain, and raced with anticipation at every little progress. In parallel with her daughter's health, Olivia's poor heart badly needed a calm atmosphere to recuperate.

Olivia signed the last discharge form, collected the prescriptions and signaled to the orderly rolling the wheelchair to come in.

"No more dizziness, *ma petite chérie*?" Luc tenderly asked. He had spoiled Melissa rotten, showering her with flowers and gifts.

"Not at all. I feel just fine. Don't worry, Papa Luc," Melissa said with a dazzling smile.

Olivia rolled her eyes. Why had Melissa taken to calling Luc 'Papa' as if she were a French girl talking to her father? There was no doubt her daughter was starved for a father figure.

What a father. Hmm, what a lover.

Navy corduroy pants and matching turtleneck enhanced the blue of his eyes and his sculpted chest. After spending last night at the hospital, stubble darkened his chiseled cheeks, and his finger-combed hair fell on his forehead. Darn, but he looked every bit the dashing French aristocrat.

Her favorite Frenchman. The only man she'd ever wanted.

Melissa had been smart enough to appreciate

him from the start. The *Papa Luc* appellation had started the day after Luc had spent his first night at Melissa's bedside to give Olivia a break and good night's rest. Then Melissa had insisted she wanted Luc to alternate the night shift with Olivia, and he'd gladly indulged her.

Olivia considered her daughter with concern. Since the accident, the girl hadn't broached the subject of her birth or their last altercation. Maybe the surgeon was right about a temporary amnesia. Or maybe Melissa had blanked out the nightmarish events of that night.

"I'm not sitting in that." Melissa pointed to the wheelchair. "Take it away," she ordered the orderly with a stubborn tilt to her chin.

Here we go. Trouble starting. Melissa felt better, all right. Her combative nature had come back full strength.

"No problem, *ma petite*. May I be your escort?" Luc bowed in front of her daughter with a flourish and offered her his arm.

Melissa giggled and hooked her arm in his elbow.

"Lean on me. I don't want you to collapse before we get out of this place. We have been here long enough." He turned to the orderly. "Can you roll the wheelchair beside us, please? In case we may need it."

Spoiled rotten. How was Olivia to handle her daughter after that? She shrugged. For the moment, she was just as happy to get out of hospital confinement.

On the cart pushed by a hospital volunteer, she arranged the dozen vases and baskets of flowers that had transformed Melissa's hospital room into a fragrant little garden. Then she followed Luc and Melissa down the hallway and into the elevator.

Outside, Luc gave a ticket to the valet. When

Olivia's van stopped at the curb, Luc helped Melissa into the back seat and arranged a blanket on her lap. "You had better stretch your legs on the seat to feel more comfortable."

"Okay."

Okay? Wow. Amazing how Luc's orders were received with a smile or an okay, while Olivia had to repeat her requests at least two or three times to get a reaction.

Had she been wanting on motherly skills?

Forget it. That was part of Luc's killer charm and the power he had over every female crossing his path. He smiled. They melted. *Disgusting*. And yet Olivia knew deep down that she loved his smile more than any other woman ever had.

"Do you mind if I drive, Olivia?"

"Not at all."

Somehow he felt compelled to ask permission whenever they rode in her car, although he never really waited for her answer as he held the passenger door open for her.

The car rolled smoothly out of the hospital grounds. Olivia's sigh of relief echoed Melissa. "Dr. Sloane told me I'd be well enough to dance in a couple of weeks. We'd better plan something."

"Of course, we will," Luc answered with a wink in the rear-view mirror. Olivia stopped listening as they chatted, more worried by the minute at the girl's lack of concern for her accident, surgery and post-operative health.

Short term memory loss? How long would it last? In a way she'd rather see Melissa with a temporary amnesia that would heal soon rather than watch her deny the truth the way Olivia had for years.

Luc continued along the narrow road where they'd found the white Cadillac the night of the accident.

"It was here." Melissa's scream prickled the skin of Olivia's nape. "The eyes. A deer. Oh God. I tried to avoid it."

"Honey, calm down. It's over. It's okay." Olivia spoke with the calm voice she used with her patients. "Luc, can you stop for a second? I need to go in the back and hold her."

Rather than stopping, Luc stomped on the accelerator and raced the car down the country road. "I prefer to get out of here."

Olivia sighed, praying that Melissa would stop shaking. Ten minutes later Luc activated the garage door opener and parked the van inside the garage. He climbed out of his seat, opened the rear door and scooped Melissa into his arms. "I can walk," she said her voice surprisingly calm after her outburst.

"I know," Luc said with a charming smile. "But you wanted to dance. We will dance all the way upstairs."

Melissa chuckled. "You're so funny, Papa Luc."

Olivia stared as her daughter laced her hands behind Luc's neck and let him waltz her through the kitchen, the hallway and up the stairs, all the while whispering something.

A perfect picture of a loving family.

This was what she'd missed for years. To think she'd pushed Luc away—again—to dedicate herself exclusively to Melissa.

Would Melissa appreciate her mother's sacrifice?

Her daughter's chuckle chimed in response as she nestled cozily in Luc's arms. The very spot where Olivia had thought she'd spend the rest of her life.

Gosh, was she jealous of Melissa's affection toward Luc?

Life's irony. Melissa might one day throw in her face that Olivia had deprived her of her self-adopted Papa Luc.

Olivia's mind spun in a whirlpool of contradictory emotions as she slowly followed them to Melissa's room.

Luc gently laid his charge in the middle of the bed. "Anything else I can do for my princess?"

Melissa sighed. "You've done a lot. I wish you could really be..." Her eyes darkened. "Tell me, did you ever meet Mom's first...boyfriend?"

"What?" Olivia swallowed a gasp. Her chest squeezed as Melissa's question boomeranged in her brain. And the way she referred to her natural father as *Mom's first boyfriend.* What was going on in her daughter's head?

Luc's smiling face turned serious as he focused his gaze on Melissa. Olivia took a step forward, intending to protect her daughter one more time from the specter of the past. But Luc raised his hand in a calming gesture. After a quick glance at Olivia, he crouched in front of the bed, his eyes at Melissa's level.

"Yes. I met him recently. He is my patient."

"Your patient? Is he...sick?"

"In a way. I am a psychiatrist. Like your *maman.* We treat patients with mental disorders."

Melissa cringed, her eyes narrowed. "Bad disorders?"

"I am sorry Melissa. I can't disclose patients' information."

"I see." She closed her eyes.

"Darling," Olivia started forward.

"I'd like to rest."

"Of course. Please, Luc, come."

He preceded her out of the room. As she was about to close the door behind them, Melissa called, "Mom, you're the best mother in the world."

Olivia darted to the bed.

"Thank you for giving me a heroic dead father for sixteen years."

Tears streaming down her face, Olivia enfolded her beautiful daughter in her arms.

****

A glass of wine in hand, Luc paced the living room in slow methodical steps, from the window to the hallway and back to the window. He paused and glanced at his watch, then toward the upper landing. He wanted to give Olivia as much time as she needed to bond with her daughter again and to knock down the wall of silence that had separated her from Melissa in the past two weeks.

During the post-operative recovery, he had studied Melissa carefully. Far from suffering temporary amnesia as they had feared, Melissa had been painfully aware of every word exchanged around her while she'd lain in her hospital bed, eyes closed. She'd turned to Luc for support, and he'd done the only decent thing a family friend and doctor could do. He'd listened to her complaints and frustrations, offered comfort and advice, and mostly convinced her that her mother loved her deeply.

He'd also returned her confidence by telling her about his little son. He groaned, embarrassed by the tears that had tickled his eyes when she'd thrown her arms around his neck and asked if she could call him *Papa* in memory of his little boy.

Regardless, he couldn't stand to see Olivia's resigned glances as she watched them chat while she stayed away, feeling unwanted by Melissa. She should be in his arms. Before her daughter or any woman in the world. If only she'd allow him...

Her slippers shuffled on the carpeted steps. Luc raised his head. Her eyes were moist, but a lovely smile brightened her face. Her first smile in ages.

Had the stubborn wall crumbled between mother and daughter? Was the nightmare of the past weeks finally subsiding?

He let his gaze feast on her perfect figure. She

came straight to him, linked her arms around his neck and buried her face against his shoulder. He hooked his hands around her. Slowly. He wouldn't move too fast. He wouldn't invade her peaceful space and see her squirm away.

Standing still, he breathed a wisp of the lemon and vanilla cologne she'd used after her bath and waited for words of love to tumble out of her lovely mouth. Words he'd been eagerly, or rather anxiously, waiting for since the day they'd revealed the truth to Melissa, the day Olivia had collapsed in despair.

"I don't know how to thank you. I told her about...my first boyfriend as she now calls Jeremy. I told her everything. And she listened." Olivia raised her head, eyes still glimmering with happy tears. "Oh Luc, she listened without interrupting."

He smoothed her hair away from her forehead and gravely looked at her. "I am so glad she did."

"I owe you so much, Luc."

An iron grip closed around his heart. Words of gratitude were acceptable, but they were not the words he wanted to hear.

"You owe me nothing, Olivia. I caused a commotion, a huge mess. I had to fix it."

"I don't know how I'll ever thank you," she breathed in a sigh.

The iron grip tightened, squeezing air out of his lungs. *Merde, stop thanking me. Tell me you love me.*

He gently pushed her away and raked his fingers through his hair. "No more thanks. We should be productive and plan the next step."

"The next step?" Her eyes widened with a hopeful shine.

"Yes, we need to bring her great-grandfather to meet her."

"Her great-grandfather?" she mumbled as if she didn't understand his words.

He crossed his arms to avoid touching her. To

avoid kissing her and rolling on the sofa or the floor. Or any other place he could find to make love to her. One last time before he rushed out of here with a quiet conscience and a broken heart.

But he still had one more task to accomplish. "I suggest you stay with Melissa now. If you don't mind, I will call Rutherford, meet him at the Crisis Center, and gently break the news that he has a great-granddaughter. We don't want the old man to die on us from a heart attack. You know the impact of strong emotions."

"You're right. I'm so happy I can't think straight." She touched his shoulder and leaned against him. "Will you tell him everything?"

Luc inched back, his jaws tightening. He couldn't afford to play with fire now. Even a careless boy learned from being burned too many times. "Just the bare minimum about his lousy grandson. You can fill him in later with the sordid details."

"I'd rather close the subject once and for all."

"I understand."

"Then I should prepare Melissa for her old relative's visit." She frowned and paced for a moment. "You know what? I really want to make it a celebration, a happy event. How about if you tell him the whole thing about his great-granddaughter without mentioning her name?"

"You mean you want to make it a surprise for him? Let him discover after he arrives here that she is the lovely girl he met before?"

"Exactly, I want to see his expression when he meets her. Could that harm his heart?"

Luc shook his head. "It's good news, and I will go about it gently. Do you want to let *him* tell her he is her great-grandfather?"

"Yeah, great idea. I'll just tell Melissa that Mr. Rutherford heard about her accident and wants to visit her. She won't have time to put the puzzle together."

"Perfect. Since it's all settled, I will be on my way. There is so much work at the Crisis Center."

"I know. You've been covering for me in addition to your own work. I don't know how I'll be able to thank you for everything you've done, Luc."

Stop it. Nom de diable. Stop it. I don't want you to come to me in gratitude.

He scowled, cracked his knuckles and nodded. "I told McMillan about the accident. He said he will return next week from California. We will be fine. See you later."

He walked straight to the door without waiting for a response that didn't come. As he turned to close the door behind him, he spotted her in the middle of the living room, her arms hanging down her sides, a stricken expression on her face.

Something was bothering her. He paused. Had he been too harsh? Should he go back, tell her he was sorry for leaving in a rush?

What would he accomplish? He exhaled loudly and shrugged. The truth was out, and she'd made peace with her daughter and her conscience. She was finally content.

But Olivia would never change.

Now, she would dedicate herself to Melissa as she'd clearly specified. There was no place for love in her life.

No place for him.

All she could give him was gratitude. *Merde*, he didn't want her gratitude.

He would finish his mission, bring the old man, and let them mend the past while he collected his suitcases and handed the keys to McMillan.

Then he would go back to France. To his empty life.

Chapter Nineteen

"Mom," Melissa called, standing in the doorway of Olivia's bedroom. "Mo-om, are you crying? What's wrong?"

"Nothing, really." Olivia sat on her bed and sniffed. "It's just a bad case of nerves after the emotions we've been through."

"I understand," Melissa said, with surprising maturity for her age. "Things will improve from now on."

"Yeah." Maybe they'd improve for Melissa who was young and had her life ahead of her. For Olivia, it was the end of a dream. She'd pushed Luc away because she owed it to Melissa to make up for her past mistakes.

But it hurt so much to lose Luc again.

"Mom, what's really wrong?" Melissa repeated as she settled next to Olivia on the bed.

"It's just that Luc is gone and—"

"What d'you mean gone? He went back to CUH to work. He told me he'll be back in a few days to check on me."

Olivia sighed. "You don't understand. Luc and I...we..."

"Mom, what if you tell me your whole story with Luc?"

"What's the point? It's all in the past now."

"Oh no, it's not. I want my Papa Luc around."

"But, honey, I gave him up for you."

"For me? You must be kidding? He's exactly the sort of dad I had in mind for years."

Olivia looked into her daughter's eyes, seeking

answers to her own questions. "What about your real father? Don't you want to meet him?"

Melissa shuddered and chewed on her lip. "I...I'm not sure I want to see my biological father anymore. He sounds too nasty according to what you and Luc said. He made you suffer. And he didn't want me." Tears pooled in her eyes. "He wanted you to have an abortion. To eliminate me. I don't want to see him, Mom. At least not now." She shook her head and sobbed. "He's not at all what I imagined."

"I'm sorry, darling."

"No, you did well. Everything you did. You saved my life."

"Thank you, sweetheart." Olivia gently combed her daughter's hair with her fingers and waited for the sobs to subside. Melissa looked like Jeremy, but she'd inherited nothing of his character.

Melissa raised her head. "Mom, do you love Luc?"

"Huh?" Olivia hesitated, and then nodded. It was her first heart-to-heart conversation with her daughter since they'd made up, and she wanted to show Melissa how much she trusted her. "Yes, I love him. I already loved him ten years ago. But I felt I had to devote myself to my little girl. I couldn't give you my hundred percent attention if I were married and had more children."

"Oh Mom, you let him go because of me?"

"I thought it was the right thing to do."

"Maybe at the time. I don't know. But now? Mom, you should keep him. Trust me, he's wonderful."

Olivia smiled at Melissa's enthusiasm. "I know. Unfortunately, I don't know if he still wants me after I told him to go away...again."

"You did? When?"

"After I talked to you. Just before the accident."

"Cripes. It's my fault then. Maybe I should talk

to him. He listens to me."

"No, please, honey. Don't."

Melissa planted a fist on her hip. Exactly like her grandmother, when Marianna was upset and all bossy. "Well, if you love him, do something. Go after him."

"Will he listen to me now? After I pushed him away?"

"Mom, you always told me that when I want something I have to go and grab it." Melissa chuckled. "You know Eric, that guy in my class who plays football? I like him a lot. I'm going to make sure he notices me. You know, the right outfit, a smile here and there, even a joke. That's how you get your man. You should do the same."

Olivia opened her mouth and forgot to close it. To receive a lesson on how to catch a man's attentions from her daughter was the last thing she'd expected.

But Melissa was right. Olivia would go and get her man.

****

A week later Olivia sat on the porch swing and rocked in a monotonous rhythm that matched her mood. She inhaled the woodsy scent of air and pine trees. Luc hadn't shown up for a whole week.

Unable to summon an ounce of energy to check on her daughter or her mother, Olivia buttoned her jacket and raised its collar high over her turtleneck. She shivered, although the weather was surprisingly mild for the last Sunday before Thanksgiving.

The aroma of the chocolate liquor torte Marianna baked with unrelenting zeal reached her through the open window of the kitchen, soon followed by the spicy perfume of hot cinnamon punch. It promised to be the perfect gourmet conclusion to the surprise party she and her mother had planned for the evening.

But the delicious smell nauseated Olivia at the moment, and she almost regretted the invitation issued to Rutherford and Luc for tonight.

Where was *her* Luc? Her real Luc.

The one who'd forced her to confront the hypocrisy and falsehood and denial she had immersed herself in for ten years.

The one who'd kissed her and held her in his arms almost a month ago. An eternity ago.

Damn it, she couldn't cope with his indifference, his chilly politeness. He called every day, asked about Melissa's health, consulted with Olivia about her own patients, then talked to Melissa. And the tone changed. Melissa's laughter rang all the way to the hallway. Olivia had been tempted to eavesdrop, just to hear his *old* voice again.

Why was he treating her so formally? She'd spent endless nights last week, after he'd left so suddenly, replaying every word they said, trying to figure out how she could have gone wrong.

Granted she'd told him to leave, but that was right after her argument with Melissa. She'd spluttered emotional words she didn't mean in the heat of the moment. Of course, he understood that.

Or did he?

Hey, he was a world-renowned psychiatrist, so he couldn't be that stupid? Although she'd heard that when it came to personal feelings, men could be particularly obtuse. Including psychiatrists.

She wanted his love. She wanted commitment and marriage. She had to do something. Go and grab him, as Melissa had advised. Get him back before some beauty snatched him. Olivia had been home on a leave of absence ever since the accident. Away from the office far too long.

Time to act, Dr. Crane.

She straightened, squared her shoulder and entered the kitchen where Marianna stirred her last-minute sauce. “Mom, go get dressed.”

“Well, you better tell that to yourself. You look like a slob. And put on some makeup.”

If only Marianna could refrain from ordering her around and chastising her every now and then. “Thanks.” She spun around to escape her mother’s lecture, but took in the cozy, warm ambiance of the living room. It wasn’t even Thanksgiving, yet Marianna had done a superb job decorating the old house. Olivia smiled and came back to kiss her mother’s overheated cheek. “Really, thank you for everything.”

Mama had done her best. *The rest is up to me.*

In her successful but laborious career, Olivia had learned that to succeed, one had to be well-prepared. Tonight she absolutely had to succeed in getting Luc back before it was too late. She would be ready for the task at hand.

“What to wear?” she mused as she opened her closet. She pulled out three dresses.

The red? Too Christmassy. Let’s not overdo it.

Black? She’d already worn black to the dance.

The green chiffon dress that cross-wrapped at the waist and had a plunging neckline made her smile. It’d be perfect with a jade pendant nestled between her breasts. She slipped it on. It hugged her hips and skimmed her knees. Sheer elegance. She spent fifteen minutes applying her makeup, a record length of time for her, and then she knocked on Melissa’s door.

“Come in.” Lying on her bed, a telephone glued to her ear, Melissa bolted up to a sitting position as soon as she glanced in Olivia’s direction. “Bye. Got to go,” she said in the phone as she snapped it shut. “Wow. Going out tonight?”

“No. But Luc called. He’s bringing an important guest.”

“From France?” Melissa opened interested eyes.

Hardly able to contain her impatience, Olivia shook her head. “From the hospital.”

“And you dressed up to kill for a guy from your work?”

“Of course not.”

A large smile spread across Melissa’s face. “I see.”

“Do me a favor and get dressed immediately. Something nice. Our guest will be here soon.”

“Okay. Calm down. I’ll be ready.” She scanned Olivia’s outfit. Her gaze paused on the décolletage. “You look stunning, Mom. Good luck,” she said with a wink.

The doorbell chimed as Olivia reached the bottom of the stairs. Marianna gestured for her to sit down and sauntered toward the door.

“Luc dear, come in. Dr. Crane is already here. Mr. Rutherford, what a pleasure to meet you. I’m Marianna Broccio.” Tripping on her maiden name, Marianna regally extended her hand to the old man. To protect their surprise, Olivia had asked her mother to hide her last name until Melissa appeared.

“I’m pleased to meet you, ma’am. Thomas Rutherford.”

“Call me, Marianna.”

“If you call me Tom,” he said with a charming smile and...Jeremy’s voice. For a second, Olivia’s heart stopped beating.

“Marianna, you look gorgeous,” Luc said as he kissed her mother.

Calm down. It’ll be all right.

Yes, Melissa would be all right. Her daughter was young. She would cope with the happy surprise. But Olivia...

Be careful. You blew it twice already.

She took a deep breath and quickly rehearsed the discussion she’d planned to have with Luc. For a change, she worried more about the frigid status quo with Luc than her daughter's feelings about her prospective great-grandfather.

Olivia forced herself to walk toward them and beamed as Luc stopped dead in his tracks, his eyes literally devouring her. Heat pooled in her stomach.

How she loved this man.

Let's go the French way with the three kisses. She followed the little gymnastics of his Adam's apple and softly swayed toward him to kiss him three times on the cheeks. His healthy masculine scent and a whisper of lime enveloped her. She let her lips linger on the freshly shaven skin, reveling in its warm peachy feeling.

Even frozen in place, Luc was the epitome of masculine elegance in his gray suit and red striped tie, worn with a traditional white shirt. Her first salvo had hit the target. He kept staring.

She dazzled him with her most charming smile and played her professional role for Tom's benefit. "Dr. Vicourt-Michelet, I'm glad you asked me to be here to help."

"*Pardon*?" His gaze skating over her décolletage, her world-renowned-psychiatrist lover appeared in mental shock and definitely in need of a lung specialist to help him breathe. He'd probably forgotten about their plot.

"Dr. Crane," Tom said. "Luc told me you wanted to be present. I can't tell you how much I appreciate your concern for my health. But rest assured I'll be fine. This is the happiest moment of my life."

"Please, have a seat, Tom." Marianna acted the perfect hostess. "Luc dear, can you serve the drinks? Luc?"

"Yes. Right away." His eyes narrowed as he recovered and strode to the credenza-bar.

When everyone was seated with a glass, Marianna passed a tray of hors d'oeuvres. A door opened and closed, like a gong in the sudden silence. Tom stood, and they followed suit, Luc stepping immediately next to the old man.

Melissa appeared at the entrance of the living room in a red pantsuit, her blond hair cascading down her back, as pretty as a picture.

Tom stared at her, smiled and whispered, "*Her*?"

"Yes," Olivia said as Luc nodded.

"Thank you, Lord. This lifelong doubting Thomas will believe in miracles from now on," the old man mumbled.

"I told you, you will not be disappointed," Luc said.

"Good evening, sir. I remember I met you at the university," Melissa politely said. She frowned, her gaze flipping from Luc to Olivia, silently questioning.

Olivia crossed her hands. *Please, let her be happy*.

Tom cleared his throat.

"How do you feel?" Luc asked him with concern.

"I'm fine. Can you tell her?"

"Tell me what?" Melissa asked.

"Mr. Rutherford has a surprise for you."

"Yes?" She smiled and sat beside the old man.

"I...I..." His gaze pleaded with Luc to continue.

Olivia nodded.

Luc crouched in front of them and put Melissa's manicured hand in the wrinkled one. "Melissa, meet your great-grandfather, Thomas Rutherford."

"My..." All gazes fixed on Melissa as her eyes and mouth rounded. Disbelief, surprise, and joy washed over her face. "Oh my God, Mister Ru...Grandpa?"

Tom Rutherford hugged his pretty great-granddaughter against his heart. Olivia's eyes filled with tears, and Marianna sniffed as the old man couldn't seem to let go of Melissa.

Luc straightened and walked to her chair. "Mission accomplished. Everyone is in good health and in need of another drink."

Mission accomplished? Not for Olivia. Not yet.

Time for round two.

Chapter Twenty

Olivia collected two plates and chose an assortment of pâtés, stuffed mushrooms, cheeses and spinach strudels. She gave one plate to Tom and the other to Melissa. "I think we'd better leave the two of you to get acquainted."

Bless Marianna. She'd outdone herself tonight.

"I'd like that very much," Tom said. "But first, Dr. Crane, let me thank you for your courage in allowing me to meet my great-granddaughter. You did a mighty fine job raising a lovely, well-adjusted, young lady."

Olivia's heart overflowed at the credit he gave her in front of Melissa. "I appreciate your compliment, sir." She still couldn't get herself to hug him. "We'll give you some privacy. Luc, let's go out to the back porch."

Marianna took the hint and padded to her haven, a contented smile on her face. "I'll be in the kitchen decorating the torte."

Now that Melissa's emotional welfare was under control, Olivia needed to concentrate on her own. And Luc's.

"Why the porch? It may be cold for you." His gaze darted to the jade pendant framed by her cleavage.

She arched her eyebrows.

He drew back at the challenge. "*Nom de Dieu*, what is this new game?"

"I need to talk to you." She was done with seduction. "Call it a last psychiatric session."

"You can come to the Crisis Center tomorrow."

"Damn it, Luc. They need privacy." She waved toward Melissa and the old man and smiled. "Are you afraid to be alone with me?"

He loudly exhaled. "You have always been a stubborn woman. Fine. Let's go out." He grabbed the bottle of Cognac and two clean glasses, and gestured for her to precede him.

On their way out, Olivia pulled a silk shawl from the closet and handed it to Luc. He deposited the bottle and glasses on the little wrought iron table next to the porch swing.

"You expect that frilly thing to keep you warm?"

Judging by his labored breath and rigid stance, *that frilly thing* was singeing his skin as he fingered the silk. And it certainly burned her flesh when he smoothed it over her back, and his hands lingered on her shoulders.

It was cool outside, but Olivia was too unnerved to feel the chill. Dark shadows of massive cedar trees danced on the endless grass, sporadically lighted by the half moon.

"Start," Luc said after handing her a drink and swallowing his.

Olivia sipped the burning liquid. Warmer and stronger, she tiptoed around a safe subject. "First, tell me how is it going at CUH?"

He shrugged. "McMillan arrived last night. He had a great time at Berkeley and is ready to lead his department again. Are you going to miss your acting-chairman position?"

She scoffed. "It's the least of my concerns at the moment."

"That is what I thought. While driving here, Tom told me Jeremy has been arrested."

Her jaw dropped, but relief jolted through her. "You can't believe how long I've been waiting to hear he's out of the way. Unable to harm Melissa, or me, or other women."

"He will be attended by the prison psychiatrist. Anyway I was about to ask for a replacement. As you can guess, I'm no longer impartial enough to handle his case."

She wanted to hug him for telling her the Jeremy nightmare had finally come to an end, for siding with her and relinquishing that case for fear of being biased. "I understand. Thank God, I'll be able to sleep at night without waking up in a cold sweat." An inner peace filled her.

"You want another drink?" Luc asked, interrupting her musing.

"No, thanks." She indicated the space next to her. "Please sit." She emptied her glass and set it next to the bottle of Cognac on the table.

As much as he craved her touch, Luc dropped onto the opposite corner of the cushion and the swing swayed under his weight.

A languorous melody emanated from the kitchen window. Elvis Presley's *It's now or never.*

How appropriate. Luc almost snorted at Marianna's old-fashioned taste in songs.

Should he try to convince Olivia one last time that she belonged with him? Now? Right away?

"Luc, I love you."

Air whooshed out of his constricted throat at the barely audible words. Words he'd been waiting to hear for a month. Fingers crossed in her lap, she focused her beautiful eyes on him.

"Is it true, Olivia? Is it true this time?" He put his hand on her arm. She was shaking. Trying to read her soul, he captured her gaze. Why was he hesitating to take her in his arms and kiss her and tell her he would always love her?

Always. He wanted always.

Forever.

Doubt slithered in his mind as he inched closer. Twice before she'd said she loved him, but never linked the words with *forever*. What about now? What was going on in her beautiful head?

"I would never play games with my feelings or yours."

"But you said the same thing when we made love." He rubbed his knuckles against her jaw. "And then, a few hours later, after you talked to Melissa, you told me to go away and never come back."

Hunger and need gnawed at his gut as he smothered his bitterness. He resisted the urge to believe her and crush her to his chest.

"I was facing the biggest crisis of my life." Her voice wobbled, begging him to understand.

"I know, *chérie*. But are you sure of your feelings?" He tightened his grip on her arm as if he would never let her go and studied her in the dimness.

"Luc, I'm sure. Absolutely sure." She nodded with strength.

He reached for his glass, refilled it and took a long sip, arming himself with patience to resist her tempting offer. He needed her to confront her feelings, to be certain she wouldn't turn around again and splinter his heart when another crisis hit.

"You also said you loved me ten years ago. Yet you told me to go away and never come back." *Mon Dieu*, those words still slashed his heart as they echoed in his mind.

"I was young, a single mother terrified for her daughter's safety."

She wriggled her hands in her lap. The nervous gesture almost undid him. A sign of weakness so alien to Olivia, especially now when she wasn't defending or protecting her daughter. He emptied his glass and rolled it between his hands. He wanted so badly to believe her.

"Olivia, there are always crises in life. You are facing another one right now. A happy one. Still, it is a crisis."

"I don't understand you, Luc. What more can I say?" She snatched her hands out of her lap and raised them in exasperation.

"Listen, *chérie*. McMillan is back. Jeremy in jail. And Melissa happy. I don't want you to say you love me just because you are grateful that I helped in the last few weeks. This is not love."

"Would you stop psychoanalyzing me?" She was back to herself, assertive and combative. "You're not the only shrink around here. I know exactly what I'm saying. I love you, Luc George. I love you, Dr. Vicourt-Michelet. Or whichever name you prefer. Are you going to abandon me? Do you want to go back to your social whirlwind?"

"No." His gaze fixed on the green flame glittering in her eyes.

Incensed, she continued her diatribe. "Do you want to take the French beauties out again and sleep with them? Is that what you want, Luc?"

"Of course not." As if he could ever hold another woman in his arms. Mesmerized, he swallowed, but his throat clogged with emotion.

"And am I supposed to do the same?" Crossing her legs, she let her skirt hike to mid-thigh and leaned forward, offering him a bountiful view of her cleavage. "Should I go on the hunt for some decent guy who may still find me attractive? Is that what you want? What you'd suggest?"

Mon Dieu, she was gorgeous, incredibly beautiful when she fought for what she believed in. And it seemed that now she was fighting for their love. For him?

He shifted on the seat, his breathing audible. "Don't try to make me jealous. You are perfectly aware of the way you affect me, but I can't accept a fling."

"Good, because I don't want a short-term affair

either. I've been starved for love for sixteen years." She flattened her hands on his shirt, branding him with her touch.

But he was already hers. He'd always been hers.

"And where do we go from here?" His heart hammered inside his chest as he waited for the answer that would change both their lives.

"Take me, Luc. Love me. Marry me."

His hand raised, clenched midway, then opened to cradle her cheek. "Marry? Is that what you really want, Olivia? Marry for better or—"

"Oh yes," she whispered as she linked her fingers behind his neck. "Yes, Luc, I want you forever."

His self-control snapped. He leaned forward. "*Je t'aime, mon amour.*"

"I love you too."

He slanted his mouth over hers. His tongue invaded, explored and caressed. His hand still encumbered with his glass, he tried to bring her closer.

Without breaking the kiss, she snatched it from his hand and hurled the crystal on the grass. He sat her on his lap and crushed her to his chest, deepening their kiss. His fingers danced on her jaw, down her throat and her collarbone. He freed his mouth and pressed his lips on the flesh of her cleavage, pushing the material of her dress as far as he could to expose more satiny skin to his kisses.

"Luc," she whispered, her fingers playing in his hair.

He raised his head and studied her eyes brimming with tears and emotion. "I like traditions. The man proposing to his beloved." As she dazzled him with a beautiful smile, he cupped her cheeks in his palms. "Will you marry me, Dr. Crane?"

"Yes, my love, I will."

"When? Next year? Next month? Next week?"

“Next weekend, right after Thanksgiving. We can fly to Las Vegas.”

He chuckled. “An American wedding for my American woman. I like this idea. After that we will have a formal wedding in France. In the chapel of the *château*.”

“Oh my. Melissa will be delirious.”

“Come inside. They have had enough time to talk. Can we announce it? Are you sure?”

“Absolutely.”

“No more secrets?”

“Not a single one. I promise. And I hope you won’t try to analyze me all day long. “

He burst out laughing. “As if you would let me. You are too good a shrink, Dr. Crane. But we will have to organize our lives and careers.”

“If you hire me for six months every year as a consultant at your *Center des Maladies Mentales*, I’ll make sure Doc hires you as a visiting physician.”

He grinned. “Deal. You are also an excellent organizer.” They would make up for the lost time by being twice as happy now, and—

The lost time? What about his lost son?

“What’s wrong, Luc? Is there something more to cover?”

“Olivia, you have a daughter. I already love her as my own, but—” He frowned, hesitating as he studied her, and then averted his gaze to the shadows of the backyard. “I never held my son. I never played with a baby...with my child. Do you think we could... I mean you would... I mean...”

Tears rolled down her cheeks, and she wrapped her arms around his neck. “Oh Luc, I’d love to have more children. I’d love to have your children. Oh my God, it would be wonderful to expect a child with you at my side, to build a normal family.”

“Thank you, my love.” Sniffling, he buried his head in her hair to hide his emotion. “I love you,” he said after he had recovered.

"I love you too. Let's share our good news with the family." She straightened and smoothed her skirt.

"Here. Let me do this." He pulled her fingers away and glided flat palms against the sides of her breasts, down her waist, cupped her hips and continued his erotic ironing on her belly. Then he groaned, kissed her, and immediately released her.

Olivia sighed. "If you didn't have the old man to drive home, I would have asked you to stay for a pajama party."

"No way. I have a daughter now. You can't set a bad example."

She chuckled as he opened the door of the kitchen for her. Marianna called them from the dining room. "We have a chocolate cake and hot cinnamon punch for our celebration."

"Is everything okay, honey?" Olivia asked Melissa.

"Oh yeah. Grandpa Tom is adorable. He told me about his grandson. I'll pray for him."

Marianna cleared her throat. "Olivia," she said with the same motherly tone. "Is *everything* okay?"

"Oh yeah," was all Marianna got from Olivia.

"Well?"

"We are more formal in France than in the U.S." Luc took Olivia's hand between his. "Marianna, may I have the honor to request the hand of you gorgeous daughter in marriage?"

"Oh my God. Of course, of course."

Olivia laughed. "Mom, you're supposed to just say *yes*."

"It's about time." Melissa sniffed. "Papa Luc told me he's loved you for ages, but you sure took your own sweet time to say *yes*."

"He told you?" Olivia spun toward him.

Melissa clinked on her punch glass with a fork.

"Kiss. Kiss the bride, Papa Luc. It's a tradition."

Luc grabbed Olivia's waist with both hands, brought her against him and gladly obliged. "Here is a tradition I like." His sweet kiss intended to please the audience soon turned into a passionate one. A clapping of hands brought Olivia down from her little cloud.

Her cheeks flushed, she cleared her throat. "Let's cut the cake, Mom."

"No rush, *bambina*. We have all the time of the world." Marianna winked at Luc.

Tom smiled. "We have a lot to celebrate," he said with a paternal smile. "I would like to invite you to my house soon."

Olivia and Luc exchanged a look.

"Dr. Crane, please don't worry. Jeremy cannot harm you. He is paying for his mistakes and hopefully learning from them."

Reassured, Olivia nodded. "Thank you, Tom. We'd love to visit with you."

Marianna cut the cake and distributed generous portions. "Luc, dear, open the champagne." She pointed with her chocolate-covered spatula to a bottle in an ice bucket.

"I also have an invitation to issue." Luc popped the cork and poured the bubbling wine. "Olivia and I would like to invite you all to a wedding ceremony and reception in my family *château*. My mother will be delighted to host you."

"Oh my God, Mom, you're getting married in a chateau? Oh my God. Tomorrow, I'm calling my friends first thing in the morning to announce it," Melissa said, unable to contain her excitement. "Can I be your maid of honor?"

"Of course, sweetheart."

"Will you wear my wedding veil?" Marianna asked, unusual pleading in her voice. "It will bring you good luck."

"Yes, Mom. I'd love to wear your veil."

Tom raised his hand. "May I ask for a special favor, please? May I walk you down the aisle?" he asked with a trembling voice.

Tears wet Olivia's eyes. Her lifelong resentment against the Rutherford men melted as hope and angst shimmered in Tom's eyes.

"I'd be honored to walk down the aisle on your arm, Tom." She came to him and hugged the old man who so badly needed love.

Tom cleared his throat and raised his flute of champagne. "A toast to the bride and groom. May they be happy for many long years. A toast to my lovely great-granddaughter who's giving me the biggest joy of my life. And a toast to my new family," he added with a smile to Marianna.

"And a toast to my beautiful fiancée and the love of my life," Luc clinked his glass against Olivia's.

As Luc gathered her in his arms, Olivia forgot to drink, forgot the family around her, and forgot her lonely years. Luc lowered his head. "I love you," he said against her lips.

She gazed at her French lover. "*Je t'aime*," she answered with a smile.

A word about the author...

As far back as Mona Risk can remember she has been an avid reader and writer. A childhood diary morphed into short stories and even a play. As a Ph.D. in Chemistry and director of an analytical laboratory, Mona traveled to more than fifty countries on business or vacation. To relax from her hectic schedule, she eagerly read romance novels or mentally plotted her own books. She was in a frigid hotel room in the Ukraine when she decided to take early retirement and indulge in writing the stories she'd been collecting in her mind.

Now Mona lives in sunny Florida with her husband. She likes to set stories in the fascinating places she visited. When she is not writing, Mona is probably playing with her adorable grandchildren, reading or walking on the beach.

The Wild Rose Press is publishing Mona's medical romances, which are inspired by the continuous struggle of her pediatrician daughter to juggle a medical career and family responsibilities. Mona's books include *Babies in the Bargain* and a three-book series, *Doctor's Orders,* about spirited doctors saving patients but forgetting to protect their hearts. *Prescription for Trust* is the first book of that series.

Thank you for purchasing
this Wild Rose Press publication.
For other wonderful stories of romance,
please visit our on-line bookstore at
www.thewildrosepress.com.

For questions or more information
contact us at
info@thewildrosepress.com.

The Wild Rose Press
www.TheWildRosePress.com

Breinigsville, PA USA
27 June 2010

240669BV00003B/14/P

9 781601 546319